The Ghosts of
Rathburn Park

OTHER DELL YEARLING BOOKS
YOU WILL ENJOY

THE GHOST WORE GRAY, *Bruce Coville*

THE GHOST IN THE THIRD ROW, *Bruce Coville*

THE GHOST IN THE BIG BRASS BED, *Bruce Coville*

SHORT & SHIVERY: THIRTY CHILLING TALES, *Robert D. San Souci*

A TERRIFYING TASTE OF SHORT & SHIVERY: THIRTY CREEPY TALES
Robert D. San Souci

THE TRAP, *Joan Lowery Nixon*

THE DARK AND DEADLY POOL, *Joan Lowery Nixon*

THE DARK-THIRTY: SOUTHERN TALES OF THE SUPERNATURAL
Patricia C. McKissack

THE CITY OF INK DRINKERS, *Éric Sanvoisin*

PURE DEAD MAGIC, *Debi Gliori*

DELL YEARLING BOOKS are designed especially to entertain and enlighten young people. Patricia Reilly Giff, consultant to this series, received her bachelor's degree from Marymount College and a master's degree in history from St. John's University. She holds a Professional Diploma in Reading and a Doctorate of Humane Letters from Hofstra University. She was a teacher and reading consultant for many years, and is the author of numerous books for young readers.

The Ghosts of Rathburn Park

Zilpha Keatley Snyder

A DELL YEARLING BOOK

Published by
Dell Yearling
an imprint of
Random House Children's Books
a division of Random House, Inc.
New York

Visit us on the Web! www.randomhouse.com/kids

**Educators and librarians, for a variety of teaching tools,
visit us at www.randomhouse.com/teachers**

ISBN: 0-440-41711-2

Reprinted by arrangement with Delacorte Press

Printed in the United States of America

August 2004

10 9 8 7 6 5 4 3 2 1

OPM

One

One

He was lost. Matthew Hamilton, known as Matt or the Hamster, was hopelessly lost in an endless forest. And, as usual, it was all his own fault.

This particular disaster was his own fault because it wouldn't have happened if he hadn't been doing something he'd thought he'd pretty much outgrown and had promised to quit doing. Promised himself, that is. It wasn't the kind of thing you would promise your folks not to do anymore, because most of the time nobody knew he was doing it, at least not exactly. What the family thought was . . . Well, the way his brother, Justin, always put it was "The Hamster is weirding out again."

Of course, if you really were looking to blame it on something else, you might say the forest itself was partly to blame. The thing was, it was the kind of forest that you read about and see fantastic pictures of, but that, if you were from a place like Six Palms, you'd never seen up close and personal. Back home in Six Palms, a hike might take you to where you could see a few scrawny palm trees and a lot of prickly cactus, but here in a place called Rathburn

Park, enormous trees marched away into the distance in every direction like endless armies of green giants. And far above, row after row of needle-fringed fingers pointed toward a faraway blue sky. A heroic forest every bit as wild and mysterious as . . . When Matt thought back over historic forests he'd read about and imagined, what immediately came to mind was—*Sherwood*.

That's what had done it. Remembering Sherwood had started Matt thinking that the forest all around him must be as incredibly dense and mysterious as Sherwood. Mysterious, that is, to everyone except Robin Hood and his Merry Men.

Robin Hood had been one of Matt's favorite historical heroes back in Six Palms, and this certainly wasn't the first time he'd done the Robin Hood thing, but somehow sagebrush and cactus hadn't been nearly as inspiring. This time there was not only this real, honest-to-God forest, but also a sturdy walking stick that he'd just happened to pick up near the beginning of the trail. A walking stick that was almost as big and strong as—a quarterstaff, maybe.

So there he'd been, leaning on his walking stick/ quarterstaff while letting his mind surf back over all the fascinating stuff he'd read about Robin Hood and seen in movies and on TV. About a guy who'd robbed rich bad guys and helped poor people, and who knew every inch of an enormous forest the way an ordinary person would know his own backyard.

Remembering the quarterstaff fight with Little John, Matt had twirled his stick and sliced the air once or twice, and one thing had led to another. Before long, although he'd promised himself to stop doing that kind of thing, he began to morph into—Robin himself. So there he was, a tall, good-looking guy, dressed in Lincoln green, running down the rough trail with a speedy, surefooted stride. As he ran, he paused only long enough to whistle a signal to his Merry Men, or to listen, hand cupped to ear, for the approach of the evil King John and his dangerous gang of knights.

Somewhere along the way the trail rose, wound along the side of a hill, and then dropped again, crisscrossing a network of smaller pathways. Pathways worn into the forest floor by deer, perhaps? Or packs of bloodthirsty, ravenous wolves? As Robin picked up his pace, his eyes searched the underbrush for the gleam of white fangs.

Flecks of light filtering down through the branches looked almost like snow. And suddenly wolves were everywhere. Robin was forced to stop again and again to fight off their attacks with his trusty quarterstaff. He swung the heavy staff fiercely and the wolves yelped and cringed before they faded back into the snow-covered underbrush.

As he ran on, the wolves and the snow were followed by an even more dangerous attack. Warned by the distant thud of hooves, Robin hid beside the trail, his longbow ready. As King John's men appeared, he released arrow after arrow and then, as the few remaining knights turned and fled, he sped on.

But in the end it was just Matt again who staggered to a stop, his imagination as exhausted as his muscles. Just eleven-year-old Matthew Hamilton, propping himself up with a stick as he struggled to catch his breath. The sturdy walking stick that had been a quarterstaff and then a longbow was once again nothing more than a prop to lean on.

But at that particular moment, a prop was exactly what Matt needed. As he gasped for air, he told himself he'd overdone it for sure this time. He'd really let his imagination run away with him. He grimaced again as he realized that his runaway imagination had somehow managed to cover up some unpleasant realities, like a blistered heel, aching calf muscles and—he swallowed painfully—a tongue-shriveling thirst. Turning back the way he'd come, he began to retrace his steps.

He moved more slowly then, glancing from side to side as he looked for something familiar that would prove that he really was heading back the way he'd come. But one tree trunk looked pretty much like the next, and a vine-covered stump was only one of many vine-covered stumps.

He wasn't lost, he told himself. Not really. How could he be, while he was still on the path he'd been following since he'd left the parking lot? On the same path—or not? It was a trail, all right, but could it be a different one? One that started somewhere else and led to who-knows-where?

The trail climbed again, and Matt began to notice other, narrower pathways intersecting it from time to time. What if he'd taken the wrong turn somewhere along the way? Maybe that was why the trail he'd been following had never passed the old Rathburn mansion, the way the guy in the parking lot had said it would. Which might mean—and this was a pretty scary idea—that he had been off course for a long time.

As the awful truth began to sink in, Matt's forward progress slowed and finally stopped altogether. Leaning on his stick, he shook his head in disgust. He really was lost, and it was his own fault—nobody else's. He grinned ruefully, imagining what Justin would say, or even his sister, Courtney. It was easy to guess what anyone in the family would say if Matt tried to blame it on Robin Hood. No way. Robin was long gone and, as always, Matthew Hamilton was on his own. On his own in another embarrassing, and this time maybe even dangerous, mess. And he'd done it on what was supposed to have been a really important day for the whole Hamilton family. A day when Gerald Hamilton, Matt's dad, was being introduced to all the important citizens of Timber City at their especially historic, traditional Fourth of July picnic.

Two

Right then, while he was still waiting to catch his breath and decide what to do next, Matt couldn't help reminding himself about the importance of this particular day, and this particular picnic. He tried not to, but it wasn't an easy thing to forget.

According to *The Timber City Morning Star,* the town's Fourth of July picnic had been going on since 1929, and it had always been famous for its great food, as well as for all the important people who attended. People like lawyers and doctors and politicians and businesspeople and members of the city council. Important people who were the ones, according to Mom, who had decided to hire Dad as their new city manager.

"But in July. A picnic lunch for stuffed-shirt types in the middle of July?" Justin had asked Mom that morning at breakfast. "Why not in some nice air-conditioned restaurant?"

Mom had laughed. "Because, as I understand it, it's an old tradition that celebrates the founding of Timber City after the original town burned down and was rebuilt in its present location. Besides," she went on, "it probably won't be terribly hot. You're forgetting we're not living in Six Palms anymore."

"As if," Justin had said. "That particular fact doesn't happen to be something I'm going to forget anytime soon." Justin, who was sixteen and about to be a junior in high school, and who had been on at least a half dozen All-Star teams back in Six Palms, wasn't a bit happy about having had to move to Timber City, and he didn't care who knew it. Giving Mom his famous sarcastic sneer, he went on, "How about letting me stay home?"

"That's enough of that kind of talk, young man," Mom had said, and then she'd gone on to lecture Justin and Courtney, and Matt, too, on how the picnic was the community's first chance to get a look at the new city manager's family, and how important it was for all of them to make a good impression.

Dad had put in his two cents then, going on about how this picnic was held in an area that had a very unusual history, which he was sure they would all find very interesting. "Especially you, Matt," Dad had said. "Sounds like it's right up your alley. And, Justin, I hear that the food's great and there's always a baseball game or two. That ought to make you happy."

Justin had muttered, "Sure. Right," and sulked out of the room, but when they were getting into the car, Matt noticed that he did have his mitt buckled to the back of his belt.

It turned out that Rathburn Park was up a narrow valley only a short drive from the part of Timber City where the Hamiltons were living. Matt hadn't seen much of the scenery on the way there, however, because he was, as usual, stuffed into the middle of the backseat between Justin and Courtney. But from what Mom and Dad and Courtney were saying, it was pretty spectacular country, with lots of big trees.

"Just look at that," Mom kept saying. "Look at those enormous trees. And oh, look, kids, a deer."

"Oh, a deer!" Courtney squealed. "I see it. I see it." Matt didn't say much because he didn't get to see much of what was being commented on. And Justin, who was still sulking, didn't say anything at all.

And then they were there, at a shady park area with lots of barbecue pits and picnic tables and, off to one side, a nice, grassy baseball diamond. A pretty ordinary park as far as Matt could see, except for the size of the trees and the way they absolutely covered the hills that rose up on each side of the park.

While the food was being unloaded and the barbecue pits fired up, Matt had looked at all the cars in the parking lot. Not that he was all that interested in cars, but Justin was, and for once he actually let Matt tag along with him and even talked to him some. Justin pointed out the Mercedes and Jaguars and even an Alfa Romeo and told Matt a lot of important stuff about which ones were most expensive and which ones he was planning to buy someday.

Matt liked it because . . . Well, for a while there, it was almost the way it used to be when Justin wasn't so busy being a teenager and a high school jock. Back then Justin and Matt used to spend quite a bit of time together, even though Justin was five years older and just naturally a lot better at everything important.

They were still in the parking lot when they ran into

this other teenage guy. Justin, who never had any trouble talking to perfect strangers as long as they weren't adults, started the conversation. The guy, who looked to be about Justin's age, or maybe a little older, had spiky hair and pierced eyebrows.

Matt went on tagging along when Justin walked over to where the kid with the eyebrow rings was draped over the hood of a beat-up truck. "Yo," Justin said, and then, "Guess you got drafted too. Like, eat at the picnic, man, or you won't eat for a week?"

The guy raised a gold-ringed eyebrow and grinned. "Nah," he said. "I came to this one, like, under my own power." He patted the hood of the pickup truck. "The nosh at this bash is to die for. Like T-bones and ribs instead of hamburgers and rubber chicken. Picnics are real big around here and most of them are the pits, but this one is top-of-the-line, foodwise."

"All right. Sounds okay," Justin said. Remembering what a fit he'd just had about having to show up, Matt couldn't help grinning, but he stopped when Justin looked at him and frowned. "Well, okay foodwise, anyway," Justin said.

Justin and the spiky-haired guy went on talking for quite a while, mostly about cars. Matt didn't have much to add to the discussion, but at least nobody told him to get lost. The other guy, whose name turned out to be Lance Layton, had just gotten his driver's license a few days before, and he already had a car.

"Well, wheels, anyway," he said. "This antique is mine. Not exactly a Rolls-Royce but it moves. I haven't gotten around to the paint job yet, but under here"—he patted the hood again—"it's really souped."

Matt could tell that Justin was impressed. Justin, who had just turned sixteen, couldn't wait to start driving, and the thought of owning his own car, even an ancient purple pickup, was probably making him turn green with envy. It wasn't until they'd said just about everything there was to say about every kind of car in the parking lot that Justin changed the subject.

"So what's with this park? My dad was carrying on like it was something kinda weird, but as far as I can see . . ." He looked around and then shrugged. "You know, looks kind of C average, parkwise."

"Except for the size of the trees," Matt piped up. "Those trees are really—"

Justin put his hand over Matt's face. "Cool it, Hamster," he said. (It had been Justin who'd given Matt the Hamster nickname.) "Cool it, Hamster. Why don't you go play in the traffic or something?"

The kid named Lance looked at Matt as if he'd just noticed him. "Nah, let him stay," he said, grinning. "I got things to tell him about this place."

Matt, who'd had a lot of experience with teenagers, had an idea what was coming next. But being teased didn't usually bother him as much as being ignored, so as soon as he could pull his brother's hand off his face, he asked, "About this park?"

"Yeah, that's it," Lance said. "Rathburn Park. The truth is, it's a pretty dangerous place."

"Dangerous?" Matt echoed cooperatively.

"Yeah, dangerous. As in, you better watch yourself, kid, or you may not get home tonight."

Matt wasn't really worried. He'd been around Justin and his friends long enough to know when his leg was being pulled. And at least this guy was talking to him. "So tell me," he said.

"Well, for one thing"—Lance was pointing at the baseball diamond—"there's a swamp full of quicksand, right over there."

"In the ball field?" Matt asked.

"Yeah, sure." Lance did sarcasm almost as well as Justin. "Right behind second base." He laughed and went on in the tone of voice you'd use talking to some kind of rugrat, "No, not on the ball field, Dumbo, but not far from it. Right out there past center field there's a place that floods every winter, and the rest of the year it's just lots of marshy stuff—and quicksand. Lots of quicksand."

"Okay," Matt said, "so I'll watch out for the quicksand. That sounds easy. Anything else?"

"Well, what do you know," Lance said to Justin, "the little dweeb's a wise guy." He grabbed Matt by the front of his shirt, pulled him closer, and whispered, "And then there's the graveyard."

"There's a graveyard here in the park?" Matt asked.

"Yeah," Lance said. "Well, right beside it anyway. You know, tombstones and monuments and like that. And next to the graveyard there's what's left of the old church. See, that's it, over there."

Following the direction Lance was pointing in, Matt saw, sticking up among the trees, what looked like the jagged remains of a burned and broken steeple.

"And on back that same way," Lance continued, "there's

what's left of a whole town, and all of it, the church and the graveyard and the town, is"—he leaned closer—"haunted. The whole place is lousy with ghosts."

Matt's interested act became easier to maintain. "Wow!" he said. "Real ghosts?"

"Sure," Lance said. "Lots of people have seen them. And there's this path that starts at the other side of the parking area. It goes up the side of the hill, and there's one place on the trail where you can look right down on a palace."

"There's a real palace?" Matt asked obligingly, even though he'd already heard about the big old Rathburn mansion, which people in Timber City called the Palace. You couldn't live in Timber City very long without hearing all sorts of stuff about the Rathburns. Lots of places in Timber City, like streets and buildings and businesses—the Rathburn Lumber Mill, for instance—were still named Rathburn, after the family that had once owned practically everything in the area. And Matt had heard something about an incredibly huge house way out in the country, but he'd not been certain where it was. Not until this guy Lance had told him.

Matt was definitely interested. He'd always liked looking at pictures of historic buildings, and he'd even seen a few in person, like the Alamo in San Antonio and four or five Spanish missions in Southern California. "Is it very far?" he asked.

"Not far at all. Maybe about a mile or so." Lance pointed across the parking area. "See those two biggest trees? The path starts right there. Why don't you go check it out?"

"Yeah, that sounds like a good idea, Hamster," Justin said. "Why don't you go do that?"

Matt knew when he was being got rid of, so he strolled off in the direction Lance had pointed. But after he'd found the beginning of the trail, he circled back to get in line for the food, which turned out to be pretty great. It wasn't until the eating was nearly over that he decided to take Lance's advice and eased off toward the path that was supposed to lead to the Palace.

Three

Three

When Matt started out to look for the Palace, he'd had to circle around to avoid the ball field, where a bunch of the picnickers were choosing up sides for a game. The baseball game was another good reason to take a quick hike. There'd be plenty of time for the people who'd hired Dad to find out that while the big good-looking Hamilton kid was practically a world-class athlete, the other one, the skinny one named Matthew, was the type that always got chosen last when sides were being picked for any physical activity.

At the far edge of the parking area Matt found a well-defined trail between two big trees and started up it at a run. He'd been planning to go far enough to see the old house and then come right back. But it was then that the Robin Hood thing had happened, and he'd pretty much forgotten all about looking for the so-called Palace.

It was just like him, letting his crazy imagination get him into embarrassing situations. Like the time when he had been doing David's fight with Goliath and wound up slingshotting a rock through the neighbor's picture window. When that happened, Justin had come up with a lot of new comments about bonehead tricks, and Matt could just imagine what he'd have to say about this one.

"Just like the Hamster, getting himself lost on an important day like this." Matthew pictured Justin's face as he said it. And he could see other family faces too, his dad's and mom's and Courtney's. Unhappy, embarrassed faces that showed how they agreed with Justin, even though they wouldn't exactly say so. At least not in front of a bunch of strangers. Matt groaned just thinking about it.

So here he was deep in the forest, leaning on his walking stick and cringing as he thought about what might happen next. Shaking his head, he lurched into a run and went on running until, wobbly-legged and breathless, he staggered to a stop. What was the point of running when he might very well be going in the wrong direction? Which would mean that the farther he went, the harder it would be for them to find him.

He started imagining another scene then. The search party. Dozens of frantic-looking Timber City citizens trudging through the forest, searching for the bonehead son of their new city manager.

In a way it was a slightly comforting thought, because with all those searchers in the woods, someone, perhaps someone with a bloodhound, would be sure to find him. For a moment he imagined an interesting bloodhound scene. An apparently lifeless Matt was lying on the ground while an enormous slobbery bloodhound sniffed at his poor unconscious face. It was better than dying of thirst and starvation, but only a little bit better actually, when you considered how embarrassing it was going to be.

What it would mean was that everyone in town would know, right off the bat, what a loser Matt Hamilton was—and probably always would be. Clenching his jaw determinedly, he started to run again, slowed to a hesitant, uncertain walk, and collapsed in a heap with his face buried in his hands.

It felt very late now, maybe three or even four o'clock. It had been right after lunch when he'd started out, drifting away from the picnic table where his dad was still talking to a bunch of people. He hadn't exactly snuck away but, on the other hand, he couldn't remember telling anyone he was going. And now that he thought about it, he realized that nobody had seemed to notice.

So what should he do? Go on running, probably in the wrong direction? Or stay right where he was and wait to be rescued—and scolded or laughed at? Probably a lot of both.

Afterward Matt couldn't remember deciding whether to go on or to stay put. At least not for long enough to do anything about it. Sitting there on the prickly needles, he made up his mind at least a dozen times to get up and start walking. But then, before he could act on his decision, he changed his mind and did nothing at all. Nothing except for some crying and a little praying, but not much of either one. Not much crying, because he really had outgrown that sort of thing. And not much praying, because the whole mess was so much like all his other stupid mistakes that he was kind of embarrassed to call it to God's attention.

Time passed and the rays of sunshine sifting down through the gigantic trees became dimmer and more slanted. Obviously the sun was moving toward the west, and if Matthew Hamilton had been anything like his brother or, for that matter, like anyone else in his family, he would undoubtedly have known whether walking west would take him back to the picnic grounds. But that wasn't the kind of thing he'd ever studied up on. He squirmed, imagining a voice, a sarcastic voice, saying, Oh no. Not Hamster Hamilton. Sure, he can tell you what happened at Waterloo, and how old Alexander the Great was when he died. That is, if anyone ever wanted to know. But don't bother asking him anything useful, like how to get in out of the rain. Or, in this case, out of the forest.

With his face still buried in his hands, Matt suddenly stopped squirming. He was imagining again. But this time it wasn't about evil kings or wolf packs, but something almost as crazy. Crazier, really. What he was imagining now was that something was coming toward him. Moving very near and getting nearer. No, not imagining. Really hearing. Something was rustling the undergrowth right behind him. And then, even before he could turn to look, he felt the air stir as it went past. Panicking, thinking wolf, or even grizzly bear, Matt jerked his hands away from his face just in time to see something—a small animal—trotting down the trail. To see a small, hairy creature move past him and . . .

"Hey," he gasped. "Hey, dog." He wasn't sure, but he hoped that was what it was. "Come back here, dog."

It stopped a few feet away, and Matthew could see it pretty clearly. It really was, it had to be, a dog. Not a wolf—too little. And not the right size or color to be a coyote. What it seemed to be was a small, dirty-white mutt, with shaggy hair and pointed ears. When Matthew called, it stopped and turned to look at him. It was panting, a red tongue lolling out of its mouth, its tail wagging gently. It seemed friendly enough, but when Matt staggered to his feet it moved away, on down the trail, and without knowing why, Matt followed it.

It wasn't until later that he asked himself why he'd chosen to follow the dog. There was no reason to think it would lead him back toward the park. Maybe it was true that he knew how to speak Dog, as his old friend, Mrs. McDougall, always said, and the little dog had in some mysterious way invited him to follow. Not that he'd noticed anything particularly inviting about its behavior. But for whatever reason, he hurried after the dog as it trotted away, and even though it wouldn't let him catch up, it stopped when he tripped and fell and waited for him.

They went on and on, zigging and zagging down the narrow trail. It seemed a long way, and yet somehow, an amazingly short time before the trees began to thin, the light increased, and there in the distance he saw the broken steeple of the burned-out church.

Matt stopped, staring in joyful surprise, and then started to run. It wasn't until he burst out into the meadow where the baseball game was still going on that he remembered the dog. Remembered, stopped to look, and found that it was gone. The dog had disappeared.

Four

Four

The dog had been there, only a few yards away, and then it had been gone. Matt was surprised at the suddenness of its disappearance, but he was almost more amazed when he walked out to the edge of the baseball diamond and nothing happened. Nobody seemed surprised to see him, and there was no special attention paid, not even by Justin, who was pitching, as usual.

The players of all ages, three or four men and lots of boys and girls, went right on playing ball. Walking past first base, Matt got a few waves and "Hi"s but that was all. Nobody said anything like "Thank God! He wasn't lost after all." Or even "Look! He's back."

In the picnic area some of the people, women mostly, were cleaning up while some others, mostly men, were playing horseshoes. A few others were still sitting around the tables, talking and drinking coffee.

Matt made his way through the crowd feeling—he hardly knew what. Relieved at first, and then confused, and finally a little bit angry. Apparently nobody had even noticed that he was missing.

"Oh, there you are," his mother said as he made his way past the barbecue pit, where the women were packing away the remaining food. "Is the game over?"

Matt said, "I guess not," and went on past. His father was still sitting at the head table, surrounded by some of the other important citizens. He was talking, and his thinnish, bearded face was wearing the solemn expression that Justin called Dad's Public Countenance—solemn, but not worried or angry. When he finally did notice his younger son, all he did was motion for him to come over, and go on talking.

"So, it seems to me that we need to ask ourselves how to apply that approach to the Timber City civic environment," Matt's dad was saying. His listeners all nodded and smiled. It wasn't until then that some of them began to notice Matt.

A big man with a kind of waterfall of double chins that spilled down over his collar said, "Well then, young man. I take it the Hardacre tour group has finally returned."

Matt didn't understand. "The Hardacre . . . ?" he was starting to ask, when another man, this one wearing a striped shirt and red suspenders, who turned out to be Mr. Hardacre, said, "Yes, sir. Mrs. Hardacre's famous local history tour. Tells people all they'd ever want to know about the town of Rathburn and the Great Fire. Mighty interesting, she tells me. Hope you didn't miss it."

Matt smiled uneasily. "Guess I did," he said. "I was just . . ." He motioned vaguely and then, noticing that they'd all pretty much stopped listening, he eased off, sat down at the end of the table, and thought about what had happened. After a while he figured it out. If anyone had noticed that he was missing, they must have thought he was either on the tour or playing baseball. He guessed he was pretty lucky—but he couldn't help wondering how long it would have been before anyone had noticed that he wasn't doing either one.

So the way it turned out, he hadn't been the family bonehead this time. This time he'd just been . . . He shrugged. Just kind of unnoticeable. A little better than being a bonehead, but not a whole lot.

So anyway, that explained it. The only part he couldn't even start to explain was the dog, and on the way home he decided not to try. He did think about it, though, without meaning to. About the dog he'd seen in the forest, and then about dogs in general. And of course that led back to Mrs. McDougall.

Old Mrs. McDougall had been a kind of neighborhood character back in Six Palms. Or, as some people put it, a neighborhood weirdo. Actually she was just a fierce-looking old lady who lived with a lot of dogs way out at the end of Bank Street. She'd had this rundown old house with a high fence around it and, inside the fence, every kind of dog you could possibly imagine. Everyone said Mrs. McDougall trained the dogs to be killers, because a lot of them ran around throwing themselves at the fence, snarling and howling, when anyone came near. When anyone came near, that is, except Matthew Hamilton.

Matt had been a little kid when he found out that most of Mrs. McDougall's dogs liked him and the few that didn't pretty much ignored him. Maybe it was because he didn't tease them by throwing things at them through the fence the way a lot of other kids did. Anyway, after a while, Mrs.

McDougall started ignoring him too instead of yelling at him to go away. And finally, after he'd been visiting with his special friends through the fence for a year or so, she began to let him inside. But it wasn't until his last visit with the dogs, just before the Hamiltons left Six Palms, that Mrs. McDougall told Matt about her theory that he was a kindred spirit and what that meant. She'd also said he mustn't grieve about leaving Shadow, his all-time favorite McDougall dog, because she was sure he would have other dog friends before long.

Even when he told her about Courtney's allergies, she said that wouldn't keep him from having dog friends in the future, any more than it had stopped him in Six Palms. Leaving Mrs. McDougall and her dogs had been one of the worst things about moving to Timber City.

Thinking about Mrs. McDougall's dogs had always been a good way to take his mind off stuff he didn't want to think about, and it still seemed to be working. Several hours had passed and Matt had pretty much put the whole getting-lost episode out of his mind before the subject came up again. The Hamiltons were all back home at the time, sitting around the table having soup and toast. Nobody was very hungry because they'd had so much to eat at the picnic, but Mom decided that what they wanted was a bowl of soup and they all should sit down and have it together.

That was when Courtney, who had gone on the tour of the ruins of Rathburn, started talking about what Mrs. Hardacre had told the people who went with her. "You know people aren't ever supposed to go there except with her tour because the land the town is on still belongs to the Rathburn family and they don't want anyone to go there except on the tour. There are No Trespassing signs all over the place. It's a really terrible story," Courtney said, "and Mrs. Hardacre knows all about it. Like who lived in the houses that burned down, and how many people died."

"Yes, dear. I think we've all heard about it," Mom said. Matthew could tell that Mom was thinking that what happened in the old town was not going to be good dinner-table conversation. Mom was very strict about dinner-table topics that were what she called unappetizing. But Matt couldn't help being curious. Except for what Lance had said about the ruins being haunted, he hadn't heard much at all. And what he'd seen from a distance, the roofless walls and ruined tower of an old stone church, didn't seem particularly unappetizing. But when he tried to question Courtney, Mom interrupted him.

"That's enough, Matthew. You shouldn't have brought it up, Courtney." She turned back to Matt. "So, Justin says you weren't playing ball." Her eyebrow went up questioningly. "And you weren't with your sister on Mrs. Hardacre's tour?"

"Yeah." Justin was suddenly interested. "Where were you all that time, kid?"

Matt didn't want to answer. At least he certainly didn't want to admit that because he'd let his imagination run away with him again he had, for a while at least, been seriously lost. Pointing to his mouth, he pretended to be chewing—chewing and then swallowing—which gave him time to think before he had to answer. Time to come up with something that would sound sensible and not be an actual lie. At last he said, "I went for a walk. On that path that goes right by the old Rathburn house. You know, Justin, the one that guy told us about in the parking lot."

Justin shook his head. "I don't remember Lance saying anything about the Rathburn house."

"Oh. Well, I guess you weren't listening. Anyway, he told me where the path started so I . . ." He paused and thought for a second before he went on. "So I went up it for a little way. But I didn't see the house, so I came back."

"Must have gone quite a way." Justin was looking suspicious. "You must have been gone, like, about two hours?"

Suddenly, without planning to at all, Matthew heard himself asking, "Did you see the dog? Did any of you see a little dog?"

"Dog? What dog?" Justin said.

Courtney, who seemed to be about to go tragic about not being allowed to talk about the burned-up town, suddenly came to life. "Was there a dog at the picnic? I didn't see it." Courtney had always been absolutely crazy over all the animals she was allergic to, particularly dogs.

But Matt was biting his tongue, wondering why he'd mentioned the dog and wishing he hadn't. Now he was stuck with trying to explain the whole thing to the family, when he was still a long way from being able to explain it to himself.

Just then Dad—who as usual had been thinking about more important things—suddenly joined the conversation. "Yes," he said to Courtney. "I believe there was a dog. I think Dr. Martin's family brought their dog. A Pomeranian, I think Mrs. Martin said it was."

"Oh, was there? I didn't see it." Courtney sounded absolutely devastated. Courtney was like that. She could get amazingly tragic about a lot of things, particularly dogs. Dogs had been one of the biggest disappointments in Courtney's life because she'd always been dying to have one, and she couldn't because of her allergies. Matt understood his sister's dog tragedy better than some of the other things she could get worked up about because he'd always been a little bit nuts about dogs too. But at least he'd been able to have fun with the ones at Mrs. McDougall's, and Courtney couldn't even do that.

"Yeah?" Justin asked. "I didn't see any dog. Where was it?"

"I didn't *see* it either," Dad said. "I only heard about it from Mrs. Martin. At great length, I might add. I think it was in their car most of the time, and she kept reminding her husband to move the car to keep it in the shade. Mrs. Martin says it isn't allowed to run around outdoors because of burrs. It gets burrs in its long hair and it bites when they try to comb them out. Yes, indeed, at this point I'm quite an authority on the Martins' Pomeranian."

So then Courtney started asking questions about Pomeranians, and Mom said they were the kind of dog that fashionable ladies used to have sitting on their laps when they had their pictures painted. So Courtney insisted on getting the *D* volume of the encyclopedia and finding the pages that had pictures of all types of dogs. Then she started having a fit about how a Pomeranian was exactly the kind of dog she had always wanted. And by the time she stopped talking, the soup was finished and Justin had forgotten, at least for the time being, to quiz Matt any more about what he had been doing at the picnic.

So mentioning the dog hadn't turned out to be such a bad idea after all. In fact, it was almost as if a fuzzy little dog had gotten Matt out of trouble for a second time that day.

Five

Five

That evening Matt waited until Mom and Dad and Justin were busy in Dad's office before he went looking for Courtney. He was hoping she'd tell him some more about the things she'd learned on the tour. Particularly the things that couldn't be mentioned at the dinner table. On his way to Courtney's room he stopped by the office to listen to Mom and Justin argue about what was making the computer say Error Type Eleven every time they tried to get it to send something to the printer. They seemed to have very different ideas about what the problem was, and what they ought to do about it, so the disagreement kept getting louder.

Listening to arguments always made Matt nervous, so he backed quietly out of the room and went on down the hall. Courtney was unpacking her animal collection, taking them out of the box and unwrapping the tissue paper very carefully before she put each one up on a high shelf. Matt watched with interest. He was very familiar with Courtney's collection. Ages ago he and Courtney had played a game called Breath of Life in which they did a secret ritual and pretended that it made the animals come to life and have all kinds of adventures.

They hadn't played the Breath of Life game since Courtney had decided they were too old for that kind of thing. Matt was sure she was right, but at that particular moment, watching the familiar little animals come out of their tissue paper wraps, he kind of liked remembering how it had been before he and Courtney got too old. He watched Courtney unwrap a unicorn made of blown glass, and then a plastic English bulldog, before he said, "Hi."

Courtney jumped. "Oh. You scared me. I didn't hear you come in."

"Sorry," Matt said. "I just wanted to ask what else you found out this afternoon. You know, from that Mrs. Hardapple."

"Not apple," Courtney said, "acre. Mrs. Hardacre."

"Whatever," Matt said. "What did she tell you about Rathburn and the fire?"

"Oh yes, that awful fire," Courtney began, but then she glanced toward the door and frowned nervously. "I think I'm not supposed to tell you about it." Courtney hated to do things she wasn't supposed to. She did them quite a lot, but she always hated it.

"Well, not at the table, anyway," Matt said. "I think Mom just thought it wasn't good dinner-table conversation."

Courtney unwrapped a polar bear made of plaster. "Oh yes," she said, nodding thoughtfully. "Maybe you're right."

Matt really liked it when somebody in the family thought he was right, even if it was just a maybe. He grinned at Courtney and decided to help her unpack her animal collection. "Here, I'll help," he said. As he unwrapped a shaggy Welsh terrier made of white porcelain that had been one of his favorites, he said, "Okay, what did Mrs. Hardacre say?"

"It was pretty horrible." Courtney raised her shoulders in a dramatic shudder. "It started in a house in the old town of Rathburn, but it was a dry, windy day and it turned into a firestorm and spread through the whole town and all of it, even the church, burned down. And some people died too. An old lady and some little kids, and a woman who ran into a house trying to save the little kids. There were rumors that the fire had been started on purpose, because the house where it started belonged to a man who had been a troublemaker, and two or three different people were accused of starting the fire. But Mrs. Hardacre says she thinks it was just an accident. Afterwards all the people who didn't die moved and started another town on land that didn't belong to the Rathburn family, and it was called New Town for a while, but then the name got changed to Timber City. And after that, nobody lived where Rathburn used to be, except for one old crazy man who lived in what was left of the church. When Mrs. Hardacre was a little girl everyone had forgotten his real name and just called him Old Tom. But then he died too and nobody lives there now."

"A man lived in the church?" Matt asked. "I wonder how he did that. I don't think it has any roof. Did you go into the church?"

Courtney shook her head. "Oh no. Mrs. Hardacre says it's too dangerous in there. We only went in as far as the narthex. That's what Mrs. Hardacre called the kind of little entry hall at the front."

"Oh yeah," Matt said. "I know about narthexes. In cathedrals and like that."

Courtney laughed. "I'm sure you do," she said. "That's the kind of stuff you always know about. Anyway, we just walked around the outside of the church and on down what used to be the main street of the town. And you're not even supposed to do that unless you're with Mrs. Hardacre. The land where the town was is still Rathburn private property but Mrs. Hardacre knows one of the Rathburns, the only one that's left I guess, and she has special permission for her tours."

"Dangerous?" Matt asked. "Did Mrs.—Mrs. Hardacre say what makes it dangerous?"

"Not exactly. Something about falling rocks and deep holes where things like wells used to be, I think."

"Not ghosts? She didn't mention ghosts?"

Courtney stopped unwrapping a large plastic buffalo and stared at Matt. "Who told you there were ghosts?"

"A guy I was talking to," Matt said.

Courtney frowned thoughtfully. "Mrs. Hardacre didn't mention any ghosts but . . ." She paused, glancing at the door. "But some girls I met at the picnic did. They said they certainly weren't going on the tour. This girl named Hannah went, 'None of the kids I know would go anywhere near those ruins, not even guys who love to do things they aren't supposed to.' And then when I went, 'Well, I don't believe in ghosts,' Hannah went, 'I don't either, but I certainly wouldn't be caught dead going where I might meet one!'"

Matt nodded slowly, his mind busy with a lot of more or less ghostly ideas. Courtney reached out for the porcelain dog that he was still holding but when he started to hand it to her something happened, the kind of thing that always happened to Matt. He let loose of the dog a second too soon, and Courtney squealed and grabbed for it and Matt did too and accidentally hit it, so that it went into the air. The little dog went way up in the air—and came down right on Courtney's pillow. Courtney picked it up.

"Is it broken?" Matt asked, expecting the worst.

Staring at the fragile porcelain dog, Courtney said, "I can't believe it. It's like a miracle." She turned the dog back and forth, examining its delicate pointed ears and skinny little tail. "It's not hurt a bit. I can't believe it. I'm so relieved."

Matt was relieved too. Big-time. All he needed at the moment was to be the one who caused one of his sister's crying jags. The thing was, Courtney had always been a world-class emoter. Dad said Courtney's temperament made him think of the Greek masks that show either comedy or tragedy, like she was always on top of the world or way down in the dumps. And she really did cry a lot for someone who was almost fourteen years old. But the amazing thing was that Courtney somehow managed to look pretty good even while she was crying. It was Matt's experience that not many people could do that.

So there weren't any tears this time but Matt wasn't surprised when Courtney said he didn't need to help her unpack anymore. At least not her animal collection.

The next few days the whole Hamilton family were pretty busy and Matt didn't have a lot of time to think. But when he did have a few minutes, like in bed at night while he waited to go to sleep, he found himself thinking mostly about dogs. About the little dog who'd rescued him from the forest, but also about Shadow and Mister and Bitsy, who had been his special dog friends back in Six Palms.

He wasn't sure what breeds they were. Mrs. McDougall didn't know either. She said she guessed that Mister was a spaniel mix and Bitsy was a husky mix, but that Shadow was too mixed up to even guess about. But all three of them had been smart and funny and crazy about Matt. He missed them a lot.

The other thing he thought about was what Courtney had told him about the Rathburn fire and, in particular, the man who had lived all by himself in the ruins of the church. It was a pretty depressing story, so Matt tried to forget about the whole thing and for a while he thought he had, but then on Thursday—when everyone else in the family just happened to be away for the whole afternoon—he found out that he hadn't. Forgotten, that is.

Dad was at an all-day seminar, and right after lunch the rest of them, Mom and Justin and Courtney, were getting ready to leave too. Mom was going to drive Justin to a baseball game and then she and Courtney were going shopping for new clothes. Mom said she needed some stockings and Courtney said she wanted to buy some pajamas and underwear in case some of her new girlfriends asked her to a slumber party.

At first Mom suggested that Matt should go with Justin to the ball game. But when Justin let her know what a bad idea he thought that was, she gave up on that one. The next thing she said was, "Well, you're quite welcome to come with Courtney and me. Isn't he, Courtney?"

Courtney shrugged and said, "I guess so. You want to come shopping for underwear with us, Matt?"

"Sure," Matt said. "I can't imagine anything more fun than choosing between roasting to death in the car, or else sitting around watching ladies trying on underwear."

He was grinning when he said it, and Courtney giggled, but Mom didn't seem to think it was very funny. When he asked if he could just stay home and maybe go for a ride on his bicycle, she sighed and said she hated to go off and leave him all alone, but a boy who got cute about ladies trying on underwear didn't really deserve to be included in a nice afternoon outing.

So that was how Matt happened to ride his bicycle down the Hamiltons' driveway at about one-thirty that afternoon and head toward Rathburn Park. Why he was doing it was another matter.

Six

I t wasn't until he was already on his way, pedaling down the driveway, that Matt began to understand exactly where he was heading—and *why*. Actually there were a couple of *whys*. The first one had to do with proving to himself that he wasn't such a bonehead after all. That he actually could go for a walk in the forest all by himself and not get hopelessly lost. He could start at the edge of the parking lot exactly where he'd started before, and then find his way back by keeping his mind on where he was going and by leaving markers at places where trails crossed each other. The other *why*, and this was an important one, was to get another chance to see the Rathburn Palace. He didn't know why that seemed so important except that a huge old house that everyone called the Palace was the kind of thing that a historically minded person really ought to see.

There was one more *why* somewhere way back in a shady corner of his mind. Another reason he kind of wanted to relive that strange Sunday afternoon. Not that the little white dog was very likely to show up again. But he had to admit that the possibility that it might was still haunting him as he pedaled down Rathburn Road and headed out toward the edge of town.

It took him quite a bit longer than he'd expected to bicycle to Rathburn Park, and after a while he began to think he'd somehow goofed again and taken a wrong turn. But he pedaled on stubbornly, telling himself that it wasn't really his fault that he didn't exactly know the way. After all, the one time he'd been there he'd been jammed into the backseat between Justin and Courtney, which made it a lot harder to keep track of the exact route they were taking.

After passing a few farms and a lot of open fields, Matt was beginning to think about giving up and heading back to town when he noticed a small sign that pointed down a side road. The sign, shaped like a hand with a pointing finger, said Rathburn Park. And right under that, Community Park of Timber City. Great! He'd done it.

"See. I'll bet you didn't think I could find it," Matt bragged to an imaginary Justin. Which was something he did a lot when it turned out he'd been right about something. Not that it happened all that often.

As Matt rode through the parking lot he could see the ballpark straight ahead and the picnic grounds off to the right. On the day of the picnic the parking lot had been almost full, but today, early on a weekday afternoon, there were only a couple of cars, and the ball field was completely deserted. Over in the picnic grounds a thin column of smoke rose up from far back under the trees, but except for that small sign of life, it looked like he had the whole park pretty much to himself.

And off to the left, not far away, but set back among thickets of young evergreen trees, he could see the broken tower of the burned-out church. Rising up through the treetops, the remains of the church had the lonely, deserted look of a ruined castle. Most of the walls were still standing, but the roof had collapsed, and what must have been an impressive steeple was now only a jagged spear of blackened stone. He hadn't come intending to visit the church, but now, as he tried to picture what it had looked like before the fire, he found himself moving toward it.

It wasn't until he had crossed the parking area that he noticed the No Trespassing sign and began to remember what he'd heard about Mrs. Hardacre's warning. Something about the fact that even on her official tour people were not allowed to go inside the church itself because it was too dangerous. Well, that was all right. He wasn't planning to go into it. All he had in mind was just getting close enough to peek in through a door or window.

There was an old-fashioned rail fence between the parking lot and the Rathburn property, but the gate was only a big yellow No Trespassing sign with a hinge on one end. It was, Matt discovered, easy to duck under the sign, but dragging his bicycle under it was a little more difficult. Beyond the gate the trail that led toward the ruins was narrow and overgrown by weeds and bushes. Matt was struggling to push his bike down the path when suddenly stone walls rose up on either side of him and curved into a pointed arch over his head, and there he was right inside what was left of the church's entry hall, or narthex, as it was called in books about cathedrals.

Something, perhaps the suddenness of his arrival, made a nervous quiver run down his backbone, and for a second or two he seriously considered making an immediate retreat. But the moment passed, and after asking himself what he was afraid of and not being able to come up with a sensible answer, he leaned his bike against the wall and moved forward to where he could see into the large open area that had once been the main body of the church. Into a very large roofless room, and directly into a jungle of young trees, huge bushes and tall ferns. At the far end, where the altar must have been, nothing remained but large piles of rubble.

On either side green vines snaked up the stone walls and spilled out through gaping window holes. It must have been a beautiful building once, with thick stone walls, a high arched ceiling and perhaps stained-glass windows. And it was still beautiful in a strange, wild way. A church for trees and vines and perhaps for forest creatures.

Afterward, Matt clearly remembered promising himself not to go any farther. What he didn't remember was changing his mind or deciding to break his promise, but at some point, for some mysterious reason, he found himself well inside the walls. Pushing his way around clumps of underbrush and large rock piles, he made his way forward enough to see, in the farthest corner, what looked at first like another pile of trash, but which, as he got closer, began to resemble the walls and roof of a tiny makeshift cabin. Only one rough wall and a roof made of rusty corrugated tin were visible, but that was enough to bring to mind what Courtney had told him about the old man who had lived right there in the burned-out church for many years.

Old Tom, Courtney had said his name was. "Old Tom,"

Matt whispered, and, narrowing his eyes, he began to build an image. To imagine an old hermit, as he might have looked during the time he lived right there, in that very spot. After a moment, Matt was able to see him clearly, to see a mental image as clear as the ones he'd always been able to make of his favorite historical heroes, people like Napoleon, or Robin Hood. Only this particular image was of a hairy old man dressed in rags. Squinting, Matt pictured Old Tom sitting at a table, all alone in his tiny hut, or leaving it to creep down the streets and alleys of the ruined town.

It was the kind of imagining that always made Matt anxious to find out more—more of the real details that would make the whole thing more alive and exciting. To know important facts, like who the old man had been before the firestorm and what had made him live like a hermit in the burned-out church. *And* what had that been like, living in such a place in summer and winter? How did he eat and sleep and keep dry and warm in a lean-to shack with no one to talk to, no TV or computer, and no way to call anyone if he needed help?

Suddenly Matt felt a tremendous urge to see inside the shack. To explore the place where the old man might have left interesting souvenirs of his life. A bed and table, perhaps, or maybe a stove or a firepit where he had cooked his meals. And possibly an old safe or cupboard full of his secret papers and personal belongings.

Matt hesitated, wanting to go on, and not wanting to. Arguing with himself. Why not? he thought. Why shouldn't I? I'm not going to take anything or do any damage. Who would care? Not Old Tom, who, after all, had been dead for many years.

But that line of thought, the one about Old Tom's being dead, led his mind off in another direction. In a direction that might not even have occurred to him if it hadn't been for what Lance had said about the old town being haunted. Lance and those girls too, the ones who had talked to Courtney about not believing in ghosts.

Matt shrugged. It was a good thing he was from a family that didn't believe in ghosts. But then, on the other hand . . . On the other hand, if there ever was a ghost . . . He remembered reading about how ghosts were supposed to hang around because they wanted to get revenge or else because they had terrible secrets they needed to tell. Secrets, maybe, about the fire and the mystery of who might have started it.

It was an interesting thing to consider. A little bit too interesting for a person standing only a few feet from the shack where a crazy old man had lived, and where his ghost, if he had one, might very well hang out. For a long time, or at least for what seemed like a very long time, Matt stood perfectly still, almost holding his breath, only turning his eyes from side to side as he looked and listened for ghostly hints. Hints like trembling moans or swirling clouds of cold, white mist.

Nothing. No movement anywhere and the only sound a soft rustle that might have been a breeze, except that there was no other sign that the wind was blowing. No movement of leaves or branches and not the faintest touch of wind on his face or in his hair. The rustle came again and Matt was beginning to back away toward the church doors when suddenly he came to an abrupt stop. Standing perfectly still, he asked himself a very urgent question. Was he still only imagining it or did he really hear a voice saying, "You'd better get out of there or you're going to get yourself killed"?

Seven
Seven

"**Y**ou're going to get yourself killed," the high, sharp voice said, and Matt whirled around to find himself face to face with something pretty amazing. Too shocked and surprised to think straight, he needed an extra second or two to make any sense out of what he was seeing.

A girl? Yeah, it was a girl, all right, but not like one he'd ever seen before. She had especially large eyes, for instance, and the colored part was extra big too so that they looked like an animal's, a wild one, perhaps, like a deer or a wildcat. What she was wearing wasn't like anything he'd seen before either. Except maybe in pictures.

The hat, for one thing. At least he guessed that was what the thing on her head was—an enormous velvety object, wide-brimmed and bulgy, covered with all kinds of shiny ribbons and feathery plumes and wrapped in a kind of veil that wound around her face and hung down over her shoulders. It did look something like the hats in pictures or movies about women way back in history, and even though it was so big and flat, it seemed to be attached to her head in some way so that it stayed put, even when the girl nodded angrily as she repeated, "You hear me? You're going to get killed."

Matt went on staring. The dress she was wearing looked old-fashioned too, with puffy sleeves and fancy frills at the neck and wrists, and a long ruffled skirt that came down to her feet.

Matt surprised himself by starting to grin. He couldn't have said why, except that a girl about his own age, no matter how weird-looking, was so much less scary than what his crazy imagination had come up with. Whew, nothing but a girl, he thought, and his grin just naturally floated up on a sudden surge of relief.

But that didn't seem to help the situation at all. The girl's frown got even more ferocious. The next words she said came out in a kind of sizzle, as if she were straining them between her clenched teeth. "What are you doing here anyway? Don't you know nobody's supposed to come in here?"

Matt surprised himself again, this time with a quick, almost cool, answer.

"You first," he said. "What are you doing here?"

She shook her head so hard that ribbons and plumes and veils swished around violently. The hat stayed firmly in place, but long strands of brown hair slid out from under it and dangled around her face. "That's none of your business," she said.

Matt went on grinning. He didn't know why, except there was something about the girl's total lack of cool that made him feel just the opposite. Kind of in control of the situation for once in his life. "Whose business is it, then?" he asked calmly.

She went on staring for a moment before she shrugged and said, "I don't know. Why should it be my business to keep a dumb kid from getting himself killed?"

Suddenly feeling a little less cool, Matt asked, "A dumb kid? What dumb kid?"

"You," she said, frowning in a way that squinted her wildcat eyes.

"You really think it's that dangerous in . . ." He paused and looked around for what she might be talking about—a dangerous-looking animal, or a rattlesnake, perhaps. Or maybe an old man. A ragged and hairy and slightly transparent old man?

Nothing. Nothing except bushes and ferns and ivy and some large piles of rocks. "I don't get it. What's so dangerous?" he asked.

She nodded. "Look, I'll show you." Shoving past Matt, she stepped over a large rock, skirted a muddy pothole and stopped. Pushing aside a clump of fern, she looked back and said, "Here. Come look. But watch where you step."

A moment later Matt found himself standing on the crumbling edge of a really deep pit. "Wow," he said. "What's that?"

"It's a booby trap." The girl's voice was calmer now, but still sharp and stern.

"A trap?" Matt gulped. "A trap for what?"

No answer.

"Who—who made it?"

She shrugged. "The old man who used to live here, I

guess. I think he used to keep it covered over with branches so that anybody who tried to sneak up on him wouldn't know it was there until they fell through. His name was Old Tom."

"Oh yeah," Matt said eagerly. "I heard about him. I heard he used to live right here in the church." He pointed. "I bet that's where he lived. Right over there. That's what I was going to check out when you . . ." He grinned. "When you saved my life. I just wanted to see it. I wasn't going to take anything, or anything like that."

The girl's glare had gone up two or three notches. Matt shrugged. "I guess I'll just have to go on imagining what it's like. Right?" She went right on glaring, so he tried a different approach. "How did you find out about it?"

Her fierce frown cooled off a little as she said, "I know everything about this whole place."

"You mean about the church?"

"No," she said, "I mean about the whole burned-up town and all the rest of the Rathburn property."

"Oh yeah?" Matt was sensing the kind of historical mystery he liked finding out about. "Why did they move the town and start calling it by a different name?"

The girl shrugged. "I don't know. Maybe the people were just kind of tired of the Rathburns—of working for Rathburns and living on Rathburn land." She began to move back toward the front of the church. Looking over her shoulder, she said, "Come on. Follow me. And watch where you step."

Back in the entryway, she looked briefly at Matt's bicycle and then stopped and looked more carefully, running her white-gloved fingers over the gearshifts and bending to check out the wheels.

"Yours?" she asked.

He nodded and she nodded back thoughtfully. Then she said, "Could I ride it? Just for a few minutes."

Matt grinned. "Like that?" he asked, making a gesture that went from the big floppy hat to the long, ruffled skirt.

"Sure. Why not?"

"Where do you want to go?"

"I don't want to *go* anywhere. I just want to ride it around the parking lot."

Matt looked at his watch. "Okay, I guess you can, but not for very long. I'll have to lock it back up before I go to see the Palace."

"The Palace? Why do you want to do that? Haven't you seen it before? Don't you live around here?"

Matt nodded. "I do now. But we just moved here. From Southern California. We lived in Southern California until a few days ago."

"Oh, okay. I get it." She thought for a moment before she said, "Look, I know how to get to the Palace. In fact I know a secret way to get there that's a lot faster than the hill trail. If I can ride your bike for a little while, I'll show you how to get there."

That sounded pretty good to Matt. A little strange per-haps, but pretty good considering that trading a short bike ride for an experienced guide wouldn't be too bad a deal for someone who seemed to have a special talent for get-ting lost. So he said okay.

What he was actually starting to say was "Well, okay

but just for a few minutes because . . ." when he stopped, fascinated by what the girl was doing to her crazy hat. She poked and patted for a moment, pulled out a long, dangerous-looking pin, settled the hat more firmly in place, and stuck the pin back in.

"All right. I'm ready now," she said. "Unlock it, please."

Thinking, This I've got to see, Matt squatted down, twirled the numbers on the dial lock and took it off the wheel. Almost before he had time to get to his feet, the girl's hands in their lacy white gloves were on the handlebars and she was pushing the bike down the path.

What Matt had said was "Just for a few minutes," but a whole lot longer than a few minutes later, he was still waiting for the ride to be over. Sitting on a tree stump at the edge of the deserted parking lot, he watched the girl ride, and the hands of his wristwatch moved closer and closer to the time when he absolutely had to start for home.

The watching had been interesting at first. With her long skirt hitched up over the bar, revealing white stockings and fancy pointy-toed shoes, and her huge hat flopping wildly around her head and shoulders, she certainly didn't look like any bike rider he'd ever watched before. And for a while, at least, she didn't ride like one. She started out slow and wobbly, but after only a few minutes she was riding much better, as if she'd ridden before, but maybe a long time ago. Watching her pedaling madly around the parking lot in sharp figure eights with her feet in their shiny button shoes pumping up and down faster and faster and wisps of brown hair and white veiling flying out behind, Matt kind of enjoyed trying to deduce some facts about her. Facts like that she'd undoubtedly ridden before but not at all recently—and certainly not on a modern, up-to-date bicycle.

But there were a lot of other facts that were harder to deduce. Like why she was dressed in what was obviously a kind of costume, and how she happened to know about Old Tom's booby trap. And why she knew a secret way to get to the Palace—if she really did. Matt checked his watch again and as the girl rode by he pointed at it and yelled, "Hey, we'd better get started."

She nodded and waved and went on pedaling, and the next time he yelled, several minutes later, she did the same thing. By the time she finally got off the bike and pushed it over to where Matt was sitting, there was less than half an hour left before he definitely had to head for home.

The girl's cheeks were flushed and her eyes looked strange, wide and even more like an animal's, or something you might see in a fantasy movie. Turning quickly away from the wild-eyed stare, Matt grabbed the handlebars out of her hands. "Well, so much for seeing the Palace," he said. "I've got to get home or I'll be in trouble."

For a moment she just stood there like she was in some kind of trance, breathing hard and blinking her strange eyes. "Oh yeah? Are you sure?" she said at last. And when Matt said he was, she thought for a moment before she said, "Well, look. Could you come back, like maybe tomorrow, and I'll show you the way then? It doesn't take long the way I go."

"Tomorrow?" At first Matt was pretty sure he couldn't, but then he thought of a way that he might be able to manage it. "Well, maybe," he said. "Around one o'clock. Could it be around one?"

She nodded. "Usually one o'clock is all right on weekdays. On weekdays there aren't many people in the park until around dinnertime." As she started off, Matt called after her, "Hey, my name's Matt Hamilton. What's yours?"

The girl stared at him for a moment, started to turn away, turned back and said, "Amelia." She was looking in Matt's direction but her eyes had gone cloudy and unfocused. "Amelia Eleanora Rathburn," she announced in a strange, singsong voice. "My name is Amelia and I live in the Palace."

Eight

Eight

For some strange reason, Matt didn't tell anyone in the family about meeting the Rathburn girl. For once he had a really interesting story to tell, one that would be sure to get everybody's attention without any embellishing, and he didn't even bring it up during family sharing time. Family sharing was a few minutes right after dinner before anyone was allowed to leave the table, when everyone was supposed to take turns telling about their day. And embellishing was what Matt usually got accused of when it was his turn.

According to Justin, embellishment was just plain old lying, but it wasn't really. To Matt's way of thinking, it was just what you do when you have something to tell but not much, and you keep thinking of all the little extras that almost happened, and that would have made the whole thing a lot more exciting if they had. It wasn't the same as lying because you weren't trying to get out of trouble or fool anybody, or anything like that.

It was Mom who started calling it embellishing, and she agreed with Matt that it wasn't quite the same as lying. But she also said he ought to stop doing it.

Dad had another name for it. He called it poetic license. Matt wasn't too sure he knew what that meant, but the way Dad said it made it sound a little better than embellishing—and quite a bit better than lying.

But that night Matt had a story to tell that didn't need to be the least bit embellished to interest everybody's socks off, and what did he do? He didn't even mention it. When it was his turn to tell about his day, all he said was that he rode his bike out to the park and back, and when Justin asked him what he did while he was there he only said, "Not much."

Later that evening, sitting on the edge of his bed, halfway into his pajamas, he wondered why he hadn't mentioned the ruined church with its dangerous booby trap, and the girl he had met there—and who she was. Or at least who she said she was.

Of course the main reason he didn't was that if he had, he would have been told what to do about it. And most of all, what not to do about it. As in—not to ever go anywhere near that old church ever again. Which would certainly complicate things at one o'clock tomorrow, when the girl had said she would be there.

But there was more to it than that. There was another reason he hadn't wanted to turn what had happened at the old church into a family sharing item. The other reason had to do with how mysterious the whole thing had been. He wasn't sure why that made a difference except that, at the moment, it was his own personal mystery and he didn't want anyone else to solve it. At least not yet.

It wasn't until he'd figured out why he'd kept his mouth

shut that he finished putting on his pajamas, got into bed and began to worry about something else. This time it was about his plan for one o'clock tomorrow, and whether it was going to work. It seemed like a pretty good possibility, but there was one part of it that was a little bit iffy.

Actually, the only uncertainty had to do with his father. The rest of the family were no problem. Both Justin and Courtney were going to be away all day on a trip to the beach with some other teenagers, and Mom was going to some kind of ladies' lunch and card party that would probably last most of the afternoon. But that left Dad. It didn't seem likely that Dad would keep Matt from riding his bike to the park, but with Dad you never knew.

Sure enough, it was during lunch, with no one at home except the two of them, that Dad started having what Justin called a Super-Parent Attack. By a Super-Parent Attack Justin meant what happened when Dad would suddenly get into finding out what his kids were doing and "who they really were." It didn't happen very often because Dad had so many important things on his mind—which Justin said was fine with him. Matt knew why Justin felt that way. There were a lot of times when Justin and his friends were doing things that definitely weren't family sharing material.

If Matt hadn't had that particular problem very often, maybe it was because he didn't have many friends who did that sort of thing. Or if they did, they didn't invite Matt to do it with them. But there had been a few times when he did something he didn't want Dad to find out about. Like when he used to sneak out to visit Shadow and the rest of Mrs. McDougall's dogs after Mom, and Dad, too, decided that wasn't what he ought to be doing with so much of his spare time.

This particular Super-Parent Attack started with Dad asking all sorts of questions about how Matt was feeling about the move to Timber City.

"I know that none of you kids were too enthusiastic about leaving Six Palms right at first," Dad said, "and I could certainly understand that." He sighed. "Your brother had a few words to say on the subject, didn't he?" Dad's rueful grin made Matt remember what a fit Justin had about having to change schools. Dad sighed again and went on, "Courtney didn't say as much, but your mother and I understood how difficult it was for her to lose a friend like . . ." Dad's voice trailed off. "What was her name? That girl Courtney thought so much of?"

"Hilary," Matt said. "Her name was Hilary."

"Ah yes, you're right," Dad said. "And I'm sure there were a great many people you hated to leave too. Old friends like . . ." He paused again, waiting for Matt to fill in the blanks.

"Oh, uh . . . ," Matt stammered, thought of saying Shadow and changed it to—Sean. That wasn't too far from the truth because there actually had been two guys in Matt's class named Sean, and one of them had been kind of—if not exactly a friend, at least an acquaintance.

"Oh yes." Dad looked a little puzzled. "Sean was . . . ?"

With his mind still on Shadow, Matt said, "Kinda short-legged. With bushy hair." Dad's nod looked a little doubtful and Matt couldn't help grinning as he considered adding, "With a curly tail."

Dad thought for a minute, probably trying to remember a short guy named Sean with bushy hair. It was after he gave up trying to remember Matt's friends that Dad stopped asking getting-to-know-you type questions. Instead he settled for inviting Matt to spend the afternoon at City Hall.

Matt gulped down the last bite of his sandwich and said, "You mean right now?"

"Sure thing." Dad was grinning. "I'm going to have to leave in a few minutes, and you could come with me and . . . Well, you could bring along a book, and there are a lot of comfortable chairs in the reception room."

"Well." Matt looked at the clock over the dining room fireplace. Almost twelve-thirty. "Well, I think . . . I think I need a glass of water."

In the kitchen, while he slowly filled his glass with water, Matt's brain raced, trying to come up with a way to make Dad forget about the visit to City Hall without having to say he didn't want to go. He didn't come up with a good excuse, but as it turned out, he didn't need one. When he got back to the table, he found that Dad had gotten up and gone to the window. Putting down his glass, Matt went over to stand beside him.

For a minute the two of them stood side by side looking out at the lawn and hedge, and above and beyond the hedge, the tree-covered hills stretching away, one ridge after the other. And then, without even knowing he was going to, Matt asked, "Dad, who lives in the old Rathburn house now? You know, the big old house people call the Palace?"

Without turning away from the window, Dad said, "Well, according to Mrs. Hardacre, one elderly woman is all that's left of the original family."

"Does she live there all alone?" Matt asked.

Dad shook his head. "Not entirely. I believe Mrs. Hardacre said that she has a small staff of servants."

"But she's the only Rathburn?"

"That's what I understand."

"And she's an old lady?"

As Dad turned away from the window he said, "Very old, nearly one hundred, I believe Mrs. Hardacre said."

"Wow," Matt said. "That is old. And her name is . . . ? Is her name Amelia Rathburn?"

"Why, yes," Dad said. "I think it is. I've certainly seen that name on some of the account books. I believe she gives money to the city to maintain the park and the graveyard. They're both on land that used to belong to the Rathburns."

They were still standing at the window looking out at the lawn and trees, and after a while Matt asked why they were doing it. "Were you looking for something in particular?"

Dad was smiling when he turned away from the window. "No, not really. I thought I heard a dog barking in the yard but I guess I imagined it." He glanced at his watch. "Uh-oh. Where did the time go? I'm going to be late. Are you coming, son?"

Looking down at his T-shirt and baggy cargo pants, Matt said, "Well, I'd need to change first, I guess. Maybe I'd better wait till next time. Okay?"

Dad patted him on the shoulder. "Good thinking, son," he said. "Well, you have a nice afternoon. Okay?"

Matt stayed at the window a minute longer, but nothing moved in the yard and there was no sound except for a slight wind-blown rustle and the soft chirping of birds. A few minutes later he was on his bike pedaling toward Rathburn Park.

Nine

Nine

t was a very warm afternoon, and Matt was sweating and puffing by the time he got off his bike and pushed it down the narrow path that led to the ruins of the old church. It wasn't until he was inside the narthex that he stopped and checked his watch. Five minutes past one. She should be here if she was going to show up, which he wasn't at all sure was going to happen. Actually there had been times, late last night when he was half-asleep, when he'd almost convinced himself that the whole thing about the Rathburn girl had been one of his crazy imagining games. Like the Robin Hood thing, for instance. On the one hand, he was absolutely positive it had really happened, but on the other—there was definitely something unreal about the whole thing, and he had lots of questions that didn't have any answers.

Questions like where had the girl come from, and how did she happen to appear in the deserted church? And why was she wearing such weird clothing? And what was there about her face and the quick, light-footed way she moved that was definitely strange, or at least kind of out of the ordinary? And another question that he definitely didn't have an answer to was why he'd gone to so much trouble to be here at one o'clock, when he should have known that she wouldn't show up.

Matt checked his watch again—ten past one now. He kicked down the stand, put the lock on the bike's hind wheel and gave the combination dial a spin. He looked around carefully again before he went on as far as the broken arch that separated the narthex from the main room of the church. Stopping there, he leaned forward, peering into the tangled jungle of trees and vines. No one. At least not where they could be seen. He waited several more minutes, standing right there in the doorway, before he took a few careful steps into the main part of the church.

Nothing. No sign of life anywhere. Outside the church there had been the leafy rustle of wind in the trees. But inside—not even that. Inside the tall, jagged walls the stillness was so deep it seemed to be a solid material, as if you could reach out and touch it. But Matt didn't want to reach out. Instead he stood perfectly still, wishing he knew if the sound of a footstep or a spoken word could reach his ears, or if it would only be swallowed up by the soft green silence.

For what seemed like a long time he went on listening—and looking. Trying, without moving his feet forward, to see if he could lean far enough to look through or around the undergrowth to where the roof of Old Tom's cabin might be visible. Somehow it seemed terribly important to catch a glimpse of the shack's rusted tin roof and mossy green wall. After a while he discovered that by standing on tiptoe and leaning to his left, he was able to see through a clump of saplings and on down almost to the corner, where . . . He was stretching out, leaning even farther, when a loud noise right behind him made him jump, stumble forward and wind up on his hands and knees. Somebody laughed.

Matt's brain registered the laugh before he jumped to his feet—and there she was. The Rathburn girl was standing right behind him.

"Wow," he said as he got up and brushed off his knees. "What was that noise?"

"I did it," she said. She clapped her hands loudly to demonstrate. *Smack!* Frowning now, she put her hands on her hips as she said, "Didn't I tell you it was dangerous to come in here?"

"Wow," Matt said again, shaking his head. "I wasn't in here. At least not very far." Then he grinned and added, "I wasn't in any danger until you scared my feet out from under me."

She didn't think it was funny. She was staring at Matt with angry eyes, but as he went on smiling she suddenly turned her face away. When she looked back her expression had changed—not exactly smiling, but pretty close to it.

The rest of her looked about the same as it had the day before except that her long dress was blue now, and the collar was square and not as lacy. The hat was smaller, too, and trimmed with braid instead of ribbons. But like the other hat, it was covered with white veiling that seemed to be wrapped around her face and tied under her chin.

Back in the entryway she stopped to stare at Matt's bike. "Okay," he said, thinking, Oh no, not that again. "Okay. When do we start?"

Turning slowly away from the bike, she said, "Start where?" She was narrow-eyed again, frowning suspiciously.

"You remember," Matt said. "To see the Palace. You said you'd show me a better way to get there."

"Oh yeah." She thought for a moment. Making it sound like a question, she said, "I guess you really want to see that crummy old place?"

"Yes, I do," Matt said, grinning again. "Really."

"Why?" she asked, slit-eyed and surly.

Surprised, Matt had to think for a minute. "Because, well, I guess it's because I've always had this thing about history. You know, historical people and places. People like Robin Hood and Napoleon. And places where historical things happened. Like Sherwood Forest—and the Alamo. I already saw the Alamo. My whole family went to see it. Seeing the Alamo was really cool."

The halfway snarl was still on the girl's face. "Well, sure," she said, "famous places like that. But the Palace is just a big old ugly house in the country. What's historical about that?"

Matt was surprised. "Ugly?" he asked.

"Yeah, I think it's ugly. And haunted. It's haunted, too. Did you know that?"

Puzzled and more than a little suspicious, Matt said, "But you said—you said you live there?"

She shrugged. "Yeah, I live there. That's how I know it's haunted."

Matt was speechless for a minute before he started to grin again. He asked, "Does that mean you're a ghost?"

Her frown deepened, turning her big eyes into long, narrow slits. "No. Of course not. It just means—that's how I know it's haunted."

Before Matt could decide what to say next she added, "And my name is—Amelia. I told you that. Remember?"

He nodded. "Yes, I remember."

"Well, okay. And your name is Matt." Suddenly her frown had changed to the strange almost-smile. "So come on, Matt," she said. "Let's go see the Palace."

She started off across the parking lot, but not in the direction Matt was expecting her to take. Not toward the start of the Palace trail that Lance had pointed out. Instead, she turned to the right, straight across the baseball outfield, moving so lightly and quickly it wasn't easy to keep up.

Almost running, Matt called after her, "Hey! Wait a minute." When she finally stopped to look back, he pointed toward the parking lot. "Isn't that where the path starts? Why are you going out here? That isn't the way to the Palace. What I heard was that the trail that leads to the Palace starts way over there at the edge of the parking lot."

"Yeah," she said. "That's the hill route. It's the way people go who shouldn't even be on Rathburn land. All they get is a far-off glimpse of the house. And the trail is, like, more than a mile long, and hard to follow."

Matt nodded. Remembering his previous visit, he could agree with that. Long and hard to follow it certainly had been.

But Amelia was still talking. "It only gets you to where you can look down and see the house from way up on the side of a hill," she said. "But you're not very close to it and there's this high iron fence that keeps you from getting any closer. This way is a lot quicker and it winds up right near the gate." She went on then, walking even faster.

Way out beyond center field the ground became rough and overgrown by berry vines and patches of heavy brush. When Amelia finally slowed down, it was at the edge of a flat open area where nothing seemed to be growing except some clusters of reedy-looking plants. Reedy plants, coarse green grass and, farther out, patches where the sunlight glistened on what seemed to be pools of greenish gray water.

"It looks kind of—kind of swampy," Matt said.

She nodded, "Yeah, you guessed it. That's exactly what it is. A swamp." She turned to look at Matt sharply. "You've heard about the swamp, haven't you?"

"Well, yes," Matt said. "This guy told me about a swamp but I kind of thought he was just trying to scare me."

"Well, it's a swamp, all right," she said. "I thought all the kids in Timber City knew about it." She turned to face Matt. "What they get told is that the public property ends at the edge of the ball field and the swamp is on Rathburn land, so they shouldn't be there in the first place. And they also hear that if they do try to cross it, they'll end up like Frankie."

"Frankie. Frankie who?"

"I don't know. He died a long time before I was born, I guess. But I certainly heard about him. What I heard is he tried to cross the swamp and drowned." She shook her finger, imitating a scolding adult. "And if you try to cross the swamp you'll drown too. But it isn't true. I do it all the time. Come on. Let's go."

"Wait a minute," Matt said. "Wait a minute."

She was already moving forward, picking her way from one clump of reeds to another. "Wait!" Matt yelled. "Hey, Amelia. Wait up!"

It was only then that she stopped, turned, and a moment later was back on solid ground. She was smiling. "Good," she said. "You remembered my name." But the frown returned as she went on, "What's wrong? Why didn't you follow me?"

"Well . . ." Matt hesitated. "For one thing . . ." He grinned sheepishly. "I'm not a very good swimmer."

She shrugged. "So what? If you fell in you'd probably drown even if you were. Nobody can swim in that stuff. You get tangled up in the roots of the reeds and they pull you down. It's kind of like quicksand."

"Oh yeah," Matt said, "I heard about the quicksand."

"But it's not at all dangerous if you're with me," Amelia insisted. "I go this way all the time and I know how to do it. So come on. Follow me and step right where I step."

If Matt had had a different kind of personality, he probably would have ignored Amelia's order and stayed right where he was. But being the youngest person in a family where everyone else had more or less alpha-type personalities, he'd had a lot of practice at doing what he was told. So in the end, he took a deep breath and followed Amelia out into the swamp.

Ten

Ten

Crossing the swamp was just about the scariest thing Matt had ever done. He didn't want to do it to begin with, and after the first couple of steps, he hated it even more. The only thing that kept him from turning around was that he was more scared of trying to go back alone than he was of going on behind Amelia. So he kept going, leaping to one tiny reedy island and then, as the one he was on began to squash and sink, on to the next.

"Come on. Keep moving," Amelia called back to him. "If you stand still, you start to sink," which was exactly what he'd been noticing. Thinking, Now she tells me, he jumped and went on jumping. At one point, far out in the middle of the swamp, he lost his balance and went down on his knees on a soggy clump of reeds. Frantically pushing himself back to his feet, he sloshed on and on until at last the landing spots began to get larger and drier. And then finally, still following Amelia, he was scrambling up a low bank and onto solid ground.

Without stopping at all, not even long enough to congratulate himself on still being alive, he followed

Amelia as she scrambled up a long slope. At the top of the slope they arrived at a high iron fence, and beside the fence a faint trail led off to the right. A trail that soon led to a grand entrance where the wrought-iron letters *RATH-BURN* formed an arch over a huge front gate. Opening a smaller pedestrian gate, Amelia led the way onto the estate grounds.

It wasn't until then that Matt looked up and saw a tower rising above the trees. A huge squarish tower, elaborately decorated with carvings, railings and strangely shaped windows.

"Hey," he gasped. "Is that it? Is that the Palace?"

Amelia stopped and turned back to him. "Yeah," she said without even looking toward where Matt was pointing. "Yeah, that's it. What do you think?"

"What do I think? Well, I think it's . . . ," Matt was beginning to say, but Amelia hadn't stopped to listen, so he shut up and hurried on, stumbling now and then as he continued to stare up to where a cluster of smaller towers was beginning to show above the tops of the trees. A whole forest of towers, reaching up three or four stories into the sky. Some of them were roundish, some triangular, some more or less square. And all of them were decorated with pillars and railings and fancy wooden trim. Matt was amazed, and very impressed.

"Well, what *do* you think?" Amelia finally waited for him to catch up. "A real mess, isn't it?"

She didn't seem to be kidding. "It's, it's really . . . ," Matt was stammering as she began to move forward between bushy clumps of underbrush. They were fairly close to the house itself before their pace slowed enough to give him time to notice that they were in what must have once been an elaborate garden. But what had been carefully planned and plotted lawns and flower beds was overgrown now and full of weeds. And he could see that the house itself was in need of repair. Paint was peeling off the bulgy pillars that supported the roof of the veranda, and here and there bits of fancy wooden trim were damaged or missing.

Matt's shiver was unintentional but not entirely unpleasant. For some reason the fact that the grand old house was shabby and run-down made it seem even more exciting, giving it the atmosphere of an ancient castle, or maybe a scene from a Halloween ghost story. He had started forward, heading toward the grand flight of stairs that led to the front door, when Amelia grabbed his arm and dragged him back into the bushes.

"Hey. Where do you think you're going?" she said. "You can't go up there."

Matt stopped. "I can't? Why not? I thought that was why you brought me here. So I could see the house."

For a moment she didn't answer. Staring at Matt, or at least in his general direction, her eyes went cloudy and unfocused. It was several seconds before she went on, speaking slowly and with long pauses between each word. "Well," she said. "It's like this." She paused, bit her lip, took a deep breath, and continued, "It's because . . . the rest of the Rathburns don't like me to bring people to the house." She was speaking faster now, sounding more like she knew what she was going to say next. "See, the Rathburns are the kind of people who don't let ordinary people come into their house."

Matt was disappointed. Still looking up at the fantastic mansion, he couldn't help sighing. He was thinking that any house with such a grand bunch of decorations on the outside just naturally would have to be incredibly interesting on the inside. Grand and elegant and full of unexpected rooms and hallways and mysterious nooks and crannies like the weird houses that sometimes appeared in his dreams.

He was still trying to imagine what sorts of rooms a house that big might have, and what they could possibly be used for, when he noticed that Amelia was watching him. Staring at him, actually, with that strange, halfway angry-looking smile on her face.

"Well, look," she said. "Maybe we could go inside—if you promise to be very quiet and do exactly what I say."

"Sure," Matt said. "Why not? It's your house."

She sighed. "Okay. Come with me. But be very quiet."

As Amelia moved toward the house she wasn't exactly going on tiptoe, but the quick, quiet way she walked had the same effect. At least Matt, following right behind her, found himself tiptoeing as they ducked in and out behind bushes, passed the end of the grand veranda and reached a long foundation wall made of brick that had once been painted white.

Amelia kept moving along the foundation until she came to an opening covered by an iron grill. Grabbing the grill in both hands, she lifted it out of the window and set it down on the ground. Just inside was a window made of many panes of glass. As Matt watched in astonishment, Amelia seemed to put her arm, clear up to the elbow, right through one of the small panes. By the time he realized that there was no glass in that particular frame she had finished unlatching the window and swung it open.

"Here. Hold it," she told Matt. "I'll go through first." And she did, disappearing feet first. A minute later she reached back up to hold the window in place. "Here," she said. "I've got it. You come through now."

It wasn't as easy as she had made it look, but with only a scraped knee and a slightly bumped head, Matt finally lowered himself down into—deep shadow, a distinct change in temperature and an unpleasantly musty smell. "Okay," Amelia was whispering. "Here we are."

Staring into almost complete darkness, Matt whispered back, "Where? Where are we? Why is it so cold?"

She made an exasperated sniffing noise. "Basements are supposed to be cold," she said. "You wanted to see the Palace, didn't you? So here you are. In the basement of the Palace. I thought you might like to see the basement first. Okay?"

"Yeah sure." Matt blinked, trying to get his eyes to adjust to the sudden lack of light. "But it's too dark to see very much, isn't it?"

"Well, just wait a minute and I'll fix that," Amelia said in an irritated tone of voice. "I just have to get my flashlight." And then, as she started away, she added, "Stay right where you are. Don't move a muscle."

"Wait. Come back. Don't leave . . . ," Matt started to say, but it was no use. Amelia's shadowy form was fading into solid black nothingness.

Eleven

Eleven

eft alone in the dark basement, Matt did as he was told and didn't move a muscle, except the ones that move when you shiver. Only a quick quiver at first, the shaking rapidly developed into something that started at the back of his neck and shook him so hard his teeth chattered. With his muscles tensed against the shaking, he strained his eyes and ears to follow Amelia as she moved away, faded and disappeared entirely. He'd gone on straining and shivering for what seemed like practically forever before a faint ray of light and the sound of Amelia's voice began to drift back to him. "Come on," she was calling. "I'll shine the flashlight back that way."

As he left the window's light behind, Matt tried to stay within the flashlight's beam, but it wasn't easy. Large dim and dusty shapes, cupboards perhaps, or simply huge stacks of boxes, crowded in on either side so that most of the time he seemed to be moving through a narrow tunnel. It was slow going. When he finally caught up to Amelia, she reached back and grabbed his sleeve. Then she turned the flashlight's beam away and began to move forward.

Matt stumbled after her as they made their way through several small rooms full of stacked crates and boxes and then into a more open area where their path wound between barrels and racks of dusty bottles. A strange, sweetly sour smell was heavy in the air. As Matt sniffed, Amelia said, "Yeah. It stinks, doesn't it? It's the wine room."

There were other dark, dusty rooms. Some where old tables, chairs, desks and cabinets sat around only partly draped in sheets of canvas. Between some of the rooms short flights of steps led up and then down again.

At first Matt tried to remember the twists and turns, but he soon realized he had lost all sense of direction. Amelia, however, continued to move forward without hesitating.

Somewhere along the way she let go of Matt's sleeve but, feeling certain that he would never be able to find his way back to the window on his own, he reached out quickly to grab the edge of her white veil.

At last, a longer flight of stairs led steeply upward to a small landing, where Amelia carefully and quietly opened a door and they stepped out of the cold and dark into another hallway and a totally different atmosphere. This hall was still bleak and bare and very narrow, but a window at one end provided at least a little natural light and the air was suddenly dry and warm. Amelia jerked her veil out of Matt's hand.

"All right," she whispered. "We're out of the basement now. Be very quiet."

As they started down the hall, Matt began to hear low sounds, which grew louder as they passed a closed door.

Clattering, scraping sounds and with them a more normal sort of smell. The warm, greasy smell of a kitchen where something had been cooking not long ago, or perhaps still was cooking at that very moment. Amelia was definitely tiptoeing now and, as she looked back at Matt, she held a finger to her lips in a stern-faced demand for quiet.

They continued to tiptoe, the kitchen noise and smells faded, and at the end of the hall another flight of dimly lit, narrow stairs led up, turned and then went up again. Finally, Amelia came to a stop, pushed open a door and peeked out. Turning back, she again put her finger to her lips and stared at Matt with narrowed eyes. "Okay," she whispered. "Follow me and be absolutely *quiet.*"

Matt followed her out through a narrow door that, as she pushed it back into place, became only a piece of shiny wood paneling. He was still staring at the hidden door when, following her pointing finger, he turned around— and froze with astonishment. They were now in an enormous room. As wide as two ordinary rooms and much longer than it was wide, it went on and on, and every inch of it was furnished and decorated in an incredible way. Large, fancy pieces of furniture sat along walls that were covered with mirrors and pictures. Pillars, statues, painted panels and curving arches were everywhere, and up above a long procession of crystal chandeliers dangled from the high ceiling.

It was absolutely the grandest room Matt had ever seen—and grand in an incredibly old-fashioned and historical way. It probably was, next to the missions and the Alamo, the most ancient place Matt had ever been in. And although the Alamo might have been a little bit more historical, the Rathburn Palace was certainly a lot fancier. Turning in a slow circle, Matt stared and went on staring, and would have stared even longer if Amelia hadn't jerked on his sleeve.

"Okay. Okay. You've seen it. Let's go," she whispered.

And Matt whispered back, "What is this room? What's it for?"

"It's the hall," Amelia said.

"A hallway?" Matt was amazed. "Just a hallway?"

"Well, not an ordinary hall like for walking through to get someplace. More like the kind of great hall people have parties in. And dance. I guess they used to have really big parties here." Amelia was sounding more impatient as she went on. Impatient and anxious, too. "Come on. Let's go. Follow me."

Matt followed her slowly down the great hall, swiveling his head from side to side as he stared up at beautiful stained-glass windows and down into huge stairwells where flights of marble stairs curved down to a lower level and up to a higher one. At last, near the end of the hall, Amelia pushed on what seemed to be another solid panel of shiny wood, and when another secret door opened, she pulled Matt toward it.

"Hey," he said. "Show me how you did that."

"Did what?"

"Opened that secret door."

She made a snorting noise. "They're not secret doors," she said. "They're just doors to the servants' hallways. All the Rathburns knew they were here. They just weren't supposed to use them. Only the servants were supposed to use them."

As they made their way down the dim and narrow stairs, Matt asked, "So this is a servants' staircase?"

"Yeah, that's right," Amelia said. "So the servants could get all around the house to wait on people without bothering anyone or getting in their way. The big stairs and hallways were just for the Rathburns."

Matt started to ask why she didn't use the big staircases since she was a Rathburn, but before he could finish the question she shushed him, pushed past him and opened another door.

This time the door led into another large room full of big, bulgy furniture upholstered in velvet and gold braid. Lamps with painted and tasseled shades and tall, gilded vases sat on marble tables, and large gold-framed pictures hung on the walls. At one end of the room was the longest grand piano he'd ever seen and, beside it, a big golden harp. At the other end a huge fireplace was surrounded by marble pillars and mirrors framed in gold.

"Wow," Matt said.

"Shhh!" Amelia thumped him with her elbow.

"Wow," he said again more softly. "Where are we now?"

"The music room. This is the music room."

Matt felt almost breathless. "This is . . . This one I really like." It wasn't, like the great hall, too huge to even imagine as a place where people actually lived. He was turning in slow circles, trying to print a long-lasting mental picture in his brain, when his shoulder just barely touched a music stand. As the stand teetered, he grabbed for it and, of course, knocked it over.

When the heavy iron music stand fell with a loud

metallic clatter, Amelia gasped. Quickly putting it back upright, she grabbed Matt's arm and dragged him back the way they'd come. They were almost to the music room's secret door when he began to hear a faraway sound. Someone was calling. Echoes of the calling voice seemed to come from every direction and it gradually became louder and clearer.

"Dolly," the voice was calling. A woman's voice, harsh and angry-sounding. And then, louder and nearer, "Dolly. Is that you?"

Opening the hidden door, Amelia stepped through, jerked Matt after her, shut it carefully behind them and hurried down the passage. Looking over her shoulder, she whispered, "Come on." Her voice quivered with anger. "Hurry up, you klutz. You have to get out of here."

Twelve
Twelve

As they made their way back down the servants' passages and then on into the basement's bewildering labyrinth, Amelia kept them moving quickly. Once or twice Matt tried to ask one of the questions that kept bubbling up in his mind, but she only shook her head and hurried on. Not until they were all the way back to the basement window with the missing pane did she stop and turn to face him. Her strange wildcat eyes were glittering again as she said, "Okay. Now what were you trying to say?" And then before he could think where to start, "But hurry! You have to get going."

For a moment Matt was tongue-tied. There were so many questions he wanted to ask. And sure enough, when he finally decided, it was obviously the wrong choice. "Who's Dolly?" he asked. Amelia's stare froze into an icy scowl and, turning her back on him, she pushed open the window.

"Go on. Get out," she said.

Matt hesitated. "Aren't you coming?"

She shrugged. "Why should I? You know the way now."

"But the swamp," he protested. "I don't know my way across the swamp."

Amelia sighed and threw up her hands. "Well, you ought to," she said. "It's not that hard. Anyone can do it."

Matt managed a rueful grin. "Anyone but Frankie?"

She started to smile and then swallowed it. "Yeah, anyone but klutzes like you and old Frankie. Well, come on then. I'll go with you. But hurry."

They were still crossing the Palace's overgrown garden when Matt caught up with Amelia, grabbed the back of her dress and pulled her to a stop. "Why won't you tell me about Dolly? Somebody was yelling *Dolly*. You must have heard it. I just wanted to know who she is."

She shook her head, still glaring fiercely. "I don't know anything about any Dolly," she said. "You must have imagined it. Come on. We have to hurry."

Matt was sure he hadn't imagined it, and somehow Amelia's angry reaction made him all the more sure it was something he needed to find out about. But for the time being, he changed the subject. His next questions were about how many servants the Rathburns had now and if they still used the servants' hallways, but Amelia didn't answer those questions either.

Matt went on asking questions without getting any answers until they reached the edge of the swamp. For a while after that the only question he could concentrate on was whether he was going to make it across, but as soon as he was back on dry land he began to try again.

Catching up with Amelia, he said, "Hey, who else lives in the Palace now, besides you? Who else is in your family?"

"Nobody," she said. "Nobody else is exactly in my family."

"Wow," Matt said. "You mean you don't have any sisters and brothers and like that?" Then, as Amelia trudged on silently, "What's the matter with you? Why won't you tell me anything?"

No answer. It wasn't until they were back to the park and almost across the baseball field that Amelia suddenly stopped, turned to face Matt and said, "Okay. Okay. You want to know everybody's secrets. I'll show you a real one. Wait till you see this. Come on."

Matt's first reaction was suspicion. Like, this particular secret would turn out to be just a way to get his mind off the kinds of questions Amelia didn't want to answer. But after a moment he began to change his mind. What changed it was something about the expression on her face. A nervous, excited expression like she had just made an important decision.

Actually, the thought of a nervous Amelia made Matt a little uneasy. A part of his mind was telling him that when a person who went through quicksand and dark basements without batting an eye was about to do something that made her nervous, it might be something you ought to think twice about doing. But another part of his mind said, "Okay. Let's go."

Walking fast, like she wanted to get to wherever she was going before she had time to change her mind, Amelia led the way across the ball field and the parking lot, and then down the path that led to the old church. In the ruined entryway Matt's bicycle was still leaning against the wall and Amelia stopped to stare at it. As he watched her run her hand across the handlebars, he couldn't help re-membering how hard it had been to get her off the bike when she rode it before. Making a show of looking at his watch, he started to say, "I don't know if I have enough time for—"

"Oh shut up," Amelia said. "When you see what I'm going to show you, you'll forget all about what time it is. Come on."

"Why? What? Where are we going?" Matt said, but she didn't answer. Turning away, she pushed aside a heavy growth of fern, revealing what seemed to be the entrance to a hidden, tunnel-like path.

"Come on. Follow me," she said as she ducked into the tunnel. She was soon out of sight. Matt took a deep breath and did as he was told.

Following the stone wall of the church, the path turned a sharp corner and went on until it reached what seemed to be another entrance. Under a smaller arched entryway the remains of an old wooden door hung crookedly on rusty hinges. The door creaked and groaned as Amelia pushed it open and led the way through heavy under-growth to emerge inside the ruined church. It wasn't un-til then that she waited long enough to allow Matt to catch up.

"Be careful," she whispered as she moved forward. "Stay close to the wall. There's another booby trap right out there."

Matt followed, watching his feet as he sidled along the wall. When he looked up, it was just in time to see Amelia pushing open, and disappearing through, a smaller door made of rough unfinished wood. And following close behind her, Matt found himself in a place he'd never been, but which was so close to the way he'd imagined it, it almost seemed familiar.

Old Tom's cabin was small and dimly lit. The wooden walls were unpainted, the roof was of rusty corrugated tin, and the only light came from two tiny windows. As Matt's eyes adjusted to the faint light he was able to see that, just as he'd imagined it, some furniture was still there. At one end of the room stood a table made of rough unfinished wood, a bench and what seemed to be the rusty remains of a wood-burning stove. And on the other side, a rocking chair with a broken rocker sat near an iron bed frame. And that was all, except that near the bed there was a large, old-fashioned trunk with a dome lid. Matt sat down on the bench and looked around.

"Wow," he said, almost under his breath. He felt strange in a way he couldn't explain. The tightness in his throat and the warmth behind his eyes were almost like grief or pain, but they weren't really either one. At least not his own grief or pain. He could only guess whose it really was, and why he was imagining it. Imagining the person who—

"Well, here it is," Amelia interrupted his thoughts. She made a kind of "so what" gesture. "You wanted to see it so bad—so here you are. Satisfied?" Turning suddenly, she grabbed Matt by the front of his shirt. "But don't you ever come in here without me. You hear?"

As usual Amelia's wild woman act made Matt feel just the opposite of what she probably intended. "Hey, watch it!

You're going to tear my Alamo T-shirt," he said, and then as she went on glaring, "Okay. Okay. I promise. I won't come here by myself."

She stared, narrow-eyed, for a moment longer before she nodded and turned him loose. "Okay. I guess I believe you."

He looked around the tiny, lonely room. "But why not? What's in here that you don't want me to see?"

"Nothing," she said quickly. "There's nothing here I don't want you to see. It's just . . ." She paused a moment and then went on, "It's his ghost that doesn't want you snooping around. Old Tom's ghost."

"His ghost?"

She nodded sternly. "Yeah. Old Tom's ghost would get you for sure if you came here by yourself."

Matt got up off the bench and started walking around the room, stopping to look at the rusty stove, the broken rocking chair and then the trunk. The trunk was made of stamped metal and it was fastened shut by a padlocked latch. After a while he came back to where Amelia was standing and said, "But you come here by yourself. Why doesn't he get you?"

She shook her head. "I don't know. Except he must like me because . . ." Another pause. "Because he knows I don't believe he was the one who started the fire."

"You mean the fire that burned down the town?"

She nodded.

"Did some people believe he did it?"

"Sure," she said. "Almost everybody did. Everybody except us Rathburns anyway. Old Tom was a foreman for the

Rathburns and they said somebody else must have started the fire."

"Wow." Matt was feeling amazed and shocked. Definitely shocked. "If people thought he'd started the fire, why did they just let him stay here in the church? Why didn't he get put in jail?"

"I don't know," she said. "I guess because they couldn't prove it. And after he'd lived here for so many years all by himself I guess they must have started feeling sorry for him. Some people in the town even had a tombstone made for his grave when he died."

Shaking his head in amazement, Matt went back to looking around the miserable little room. His eyes stopped at the trunk and he went back to look at it more closely. The padlock that held it shut looked newer and shinier than the trunk itself and, for that matter, newer than anything else in the whole room.

He was kneeling down, running his fingers over the lock, when Amelia said, "Come on. You still haven't seen the tombstone the town made for Old Tom. Let's go!" Grabbing his shirt again, she pulled him to his feet.

Suddenly Matt was tired of being jerked around. He felt like telling her so, and he probably would have if she hadn't been pulling so hard on the back of his shirt that it was about to strangle him. By the time he got his breath and voice back she was out the door and there was nothing to do but follow.

Unlike what remained of the old town of Rathburn, the graveyard seemed to be pretty well maintained. At least the grass seemed to have been mowed fairly recently, and there were wilted bouquets on some of the graves. When he asked Amelia why that was, she said, "Well, sure. That's because the graveyard and the park belong to the town, and all the rest of it still belongs to the Rathburns. And they won't . . ." She paused a moment and then went on, "And we won't let anybody change anything. Not ever. Not anything. Rathburns want everything to be the way it always was. Get it?"

Matt said he got it and went on following Amelia as she passed up all the well-tended plots and dropped to her knees in a weed-grown corner. Pushing the weeds away from a moss-covered slab of stone, she whispered, "Look." She was pointing to the words that were carved into the stone. "See. It says here 'Thomas A. McHenry. Born 1881. Died 1949.' That's him. That's Old Tom."

A shiver crawled up the back of Matt's neck. He guessed Amelia was right about who was buried there, but as far as he could tell, it was almost impossible to read the moss-covered letters. He was moving closer when his knee bumped something under a tangle of undergrowth. Pushing aside the weeds and vines, he uncovered what seemed to be a much smaller gravestone. "Hey," he said. "Here's another one. Who's buried here?"

Amelia crawled over to look. "I don't know," she said. "What does it say?"

The smaller gravestone was chipped and stained and covered with greenish moss. There were parts of letters, but it was hard to tell what they had once said. As Matt scratched at the moss with his fingernails, he was beginning to imagine the person who was buried there. A child, perhaps, under such a small stone, or even a baby. A baby—Old Tom's, perhaps? Another mystery, it seemed.

Suddenly Amelia stood up. "Come on," she said. "Let's go."

Matt got to his feet slowly. "Where? Where are we going now?"

No answer, but as Amelia led the way back across the parking lot Matt began to catch on. Began to think he knew where they were going—and also why. Sure enough, the "where" turned out to be the old church—and the "why" was . . .

"I want to ride the bike again," Amelia said. "Just for a few minutes."

"Well." Matt was thinking about saying no, just to see what would happen, but then he had an interesting idea. "How about if we make a little deal?"

Amelia's "What kind of deal?" sounded suspicious.

"You get to ride my bike if first off I get to ask you one question, and you have to promise to answer it. Okay?"

That took some thinking about, some narrow-eyed, tight-lipped thinking. But at last she opened her eyes wide and nodded. So Matt looked into those wide eyes and asked again, "Who is Dolly?"

No answer. At least none for so long that Matt was sure there wasn't going to be one. But at last Amelia began to nod slowly and thoughtfully. "I told you," she said. "There isn't anyone named Dolly." She stopped talking, thought for a moment, and then went on, "No person anyway. Dolly is just a ghost."

Matt had seen that kind of superinnocent look before

and his experience had been that when Courtney, and other female types, opened their eyes especially wide they were usually trying to fool somebody. So while Amelia rode his bicycle around the parking lot, Matt could only wonder what she was trying to fool him about, and why.

Thirteen
Thirteen

The title of the book was *Timber City, Phoenix of the Northwest,* and the author's name was Oscar Harrington. It was only a dog-eared, discolored paperback, but when Matt asked for something about the history of the town the librarian knew just where to find it. The librarian, whose name was Mrs. Keeler, also remembered meeting Matt when he'd been in to sign up for a library card. "You're new in town, aren't you?" she said. And when he said he was, she said, "And you're already reading up on the history of your new hometown. I think that's wonderful." She went on chatting then, asking him how he liked living in Timber City.

That was when Matt started telling her that he'd already found out a lot of interesting things about the history of Timber City, and how he'd always been interested in historical people and places. But he'd hardly gotten started about the Alamo when she said she hoped he'd be very happy in his new home, and went back to working on the computer.

It turned out that the book couldn't be checked out

except by adults, so Matt sat down at a table near Mrs. Keeler's desk and started to read. When she seemed to be finished with the computer, he went back to tell her that Phoenix was actually the capital of Arizona, and he wondered why Mr. Oscar Harrington, the author, had called Timber City the Phoenix of the Northwest. That was when she told him a lot of interesting stuff about how the phoenix was a mythical bird that got burned up and then rose alive from its own ashes. Mrs. Keeler said that was what Timber City had done after the great fire and that Matt could find out all about it by reading the rest of Mr. Harrington's book.

Matt sat down again and went back to reading. The book started out with a lot of chapters about how the first Albert Rathburn had come to California during the gold rush and then moved north and used the gold he'd found to buy timberland. Matt skimmed over a lot of pages about how successful Mr. Rathburn had been and how the original town had grown up right around his lumber mill. There was, however, one sentence in that part of the book that really got his attention. And that was the one that said that Albert Rathburn had married Amelia Dutton in 1861.

Amelia. Certainly not the bicycle rider, and not even the old lady he'd heard about who was almost one hundred years old and was still living in the Palace. It didn't take much mathematical ability to figure out that any Amelia who got married in 1861 wasn't in the Palace any longer. At least not *living* in it.

Then there was a short chapter called "The Rathburn Palace." It started out by explaining how people had started calling it the Palace because it was so much bigger than any house most of the local people had ever seen. After that there was a long section about the kinds of wood that had been used to build it, and all the workers who came from foreign countries to carve the wood and make things like statues and stained-glass windows.

Matt skimmed over some of the details about the Palace, but he started reading more carefully when he came to a chapter about the fire. But all it said was that a fire had started on a very hot, windy day in 1928 and the entire town of Rathburn had burned down. And that was about all, except that the town was rebuilt a few miles away and its name was changed to Timber City.

At the end of the book it said that the Rathburn family still owned the land where the old town had been, except for a few acres that they'd donated to the city for a grave-yard and a public park. There wasn't any mention of a man called Old Tom, or Thomas McHenry, either.

Matt was disappointed. When Mrs. Keeler asked him how he'd liked the book he said it was okay, but . . . And when she asked, "But . . . ?" he said, "There wasn't any-thing in it about a person called Old Tom."

"Oh, you've heard about Old Tom already?" Mrs. Keeler was smiling. "Everyone seems to sooner or later. Everyone talks about Old Tom, but I guess he wasn't the kind of person who gets written about by serious histori-ans like Mr. Harrington."

"Everybody knows about him?" Matt asked.

"Well, maybe not all the new people in town," Mrs. Keeler said. "After all, he's been dead for more than fifty years. But the old-timers certainly remember him. He was a foreman at the old Rathburn lumber mill, you know."

"Yes, I heard that," Matt said. "And that some people blamed him for the fire. The one that burned down the whole town. Like they thought he started it or something. Why did they think he'd do something like that?"

Mrs. Keeler had to go away then to check out some books, but when she returned she said that nobody really knew how the fire started, but a strike had been going on and there were a lot of hard feelings on both sides.

"A strike?" Matt asked.

"Yes, an argument between the Rathburns and the millworkers and lumberjacks. There was a man named Jansen who was a union organizer, and some people thought it was his fault the strike was happening, and then the fire started at his house. And because Tom McHenry worked for the Rathburns, there were rumors that the Rathburns had told him to set fire to Mr. Jansen's house to make him leave town. But then, while the Jansen house was still burning, a terrible windstorm blew up and the fire spread and kept on spreading and eventually the whole town burned."

"Wow," Matt said. "Do you think he did it? Old Tom, I mean? Did you think he was the kind of person who would do a thing like that?"

Mrs. Keeler smiled. "I'm not quite old enough to remember much about Old Tom. He died when I was hardly more than a baby." Her smile faded into a hazy, daydreamy expression. "I do remember Rover, though. I must have been almost your age when Rover died."

"Rover?" Matt didn't have any idea what Mrs. Keeler was talking about, but right that very minute, the minute he heard the name Rover for the first time, he had a kind of premonition that he was about to find out something very important.

"Yes. I guess you didn't hear about Old Tom's dog," Mrs. Keeler was saying. "He lived for quite a few years after his master died. At the time everyone in town knew Rover. Lots of people fed him when he came into town, but after he ate he always disappeared."

"Wow," Matt whispered as the shadowy beginnings of some weird ideas started forming in the corners of his mind. "He just disappeared?"

Just about then an impatient-type man came up to the desk and Mrs. Keeler went off to help him look for a book. She was gone quite a long time and while she was away, Matt just stood there leaning on the desk and staring into space while he thought about dogs that disappeared. Like, for instance, the small, bushy-haired dog that rescued him from the forest and then—just disappeared.

As soon as Mrs. Keeler came back, he started trying to ask about the dog, but other people kept interrupting. He was getting pretty impatient himself by the time he finally got her attention, and when he said, "Mrs. Keeler. How did the dog disappear?" she said, "Dear me, Matthew. Don't shout."

So he said he was sorry, and after she finally had a chance to listen to his question Mrs. Keeler laughed and said, "I didn't mean that he just disappeared into thin air. I only meant that he insisted on going back to wherever he'd been living. A lot of people felt sorry for him and would have given him a home, but he just wouldn't stay. The rumor was that he went back to sleep on his master's grave, but I knew some young men who said they'd gone to the graveyard to look and he wasn't there."

Matt nodded. "He wasn't there," he repeated. "Not there on Old Tom's grave, because he . . ."

"Yes?" Mrs. Keeler asked.

Matt shrugged. "I don't know," he mumbled, but he did have a pretty good idea. A mental picture, actually. An extremely clear and vivid picture of Rover sitting beside the cot in Old Tom's cabin. Sitting there with his chin resting on the edge of an empty bed. The picture was amazingly clear and full of detail and for some reason thinking about it made his eyes get hot and gave him a tight feeling in his throat.

Mrs. Keeler went off then to take care of a little girl who was checking out a lot of picture books and it wasn't until quite a while later that Matt had a chance to ask, "But what finally happened to Rover?" Because of the tightness in his throat the words came out a little raspy. "Did he just die out there in Old Tom's . . . wherever it was he went?"

She shook her head slowly. "Let me think. It happened such a long time ago." After a moment she went on, "I remember now. He died right here in town. One day he came into town as usual and lay down on the sidewalk and died. And a group of his special admirers took him out and buried him near his master's grave. At the time it was quite a well-known local event."

Her eyes had gone hazy again as she continued on, "Oh yes, and some children took up a collection to buy a little tombstone for his grave. I'd almost forgotten about that."

Mrs. Keeler got busy then with other people and Matt went out, climbed on his bicycle and headed for home. He went on thinking and wondering about all of it—about

Amelia and the Palace and Old Tom, and about the little gravestone next to where Old Tom was buried that must have been Rover's. And most of all about the strangely clear and detailed mental picture that kept coming back every time he thought about what had happened to the dog named Rover after his master died.

On Saturday after he finished his chores, Matt got permission to go for a ride before he was even certain just where he was going. What he really wanted to do was visit Old Tom's cabin, but he knew that would be impossible on the weekend when Rathburn Park was sure to be full of ball games and picnickers. Not to mention the fact that he'd promised Amelia he wouldn't go there by himself.

So he wound up at the library again, which turned out to be wasted effort because Mrs. Keeler wasn't there. On his way home he took a different route. One that went right past the Timber City middle school.

The building itself looked a lot different from the middle school back in Six Palms. Ivy-covered wooden walls, for instance, instead of palm trees and adobe. But did that mean it would be any different for Matthew Hamilton? Would he still be the last one to get chosen for teams and classroom committees, for instance? And the first one to be chosen when the jocks were looking for someone to push around and make fun of?

While he was standing there leaning on his bike, something, maybe the nice, cool summer weather as compared to summers in Six Palms, made him start imagining that maybe there would be some differences besides the weather. Differences like a few people who didn't care whether a guy was a red-hot athlete—or not. For a moment he let himself go so far as to imagine a Timber City Matthew Hamilton who got elected to class offices, and who could talk to the most popular girls without getting twitchy and tongue-tied. He went on imagining the heroic new Matthew Hamilton for several minutes before he sighed and said, "Fat chance," right out loud, got back on his bike and headed for home.

As he pedaled toward home, he was still in the midst of some fairly gloomy thoughts about school when he passed the turn-off to Rathburn Park. Passed the road that led to the park and also to Old Tom's cabin, and there it was again, the mysteriously sharp and clear image of a sad-faced dog sitting by an empty bed. And right then, pedaling along Birch Street, he suddenly remembered where he'd seen that picture before.

Fourteen

Fourteen

What hit Matt right between the eyes on his way home from the middle school that Saturday was a memory that explained the mental picture he'd been seeing every time he thought about Rover and Old Tom. Instead of an imagined image, he'd actually been remembering a real picture, an oil painting in a beautiful gold frame that he'd seen somewhere . . . And then he knew. It had been in Mrs. McDougall's house, back in Six Palms.

Nearly every picture in Mrs. McDougall's house had dogs in it. But this one was in an especially fancy frame and it showed a dog sitting beside an empty bed in a small, messy room. The dog's chin was resting on the edge of the bed and its face was very sad. Mrs. McDougall said it was a copy of a famous painting of a dog grieving for its dead master.

Remembering that painting was fascinating. So fascinating, in fact, that for several minutes Matt had a hard time keeping his mind on what he was doing, or even where he was going. He turned right instead of left on Woodland and then went right through the stop sign on Sierra Avenue without even seeing it. It didn't quite cause an accident, but a big lumber truck really blasted him with its horn.

So Saturday turned out to be a nothing sort of day, except for remembering Mrs. McDougall's painting, and almost getting run over by a lumber truck. And then came Sunday and church. The Hamiltons went to church most Sundays, which, during the summer when there was no youth service, meant sitting through the whole thing, including the sermon. But on that particular Sunday, the only Hamilton kids present were Courtney and Matt himself. No Justin.

Afterward, when Matt asked where Justin had been, Dad only shook his head and said Justin was at home. Then he patted Matt on the shoulder and said he'd tell him about it later. He was smiling when he said it, but there was something about the smile that didn't look quite normal.

Matt spent most of the afternoon in his own room writing a letter to Mrs. McDougall. He'd been meaning to write to her before to ask how she was, and how Shadow and the other dogs were doing, but remembering about the painting really got him started. Once he began to write, he got into telling about Rathburn and the man who lived in a shack in the ruins of an old church and how his dog, whose name was Rover, went on living there all alone after his master died. He finished the letter by writing, "When I heard about Rover I started thinking about that picture in your front room. The one about the dog whose master was dead. I don't know what Rover looked like, but I sort of imagine him looking like the dog in your painting."

Even though Matt was pretty much into letter writing

that afternoon he couldn't help stopping now and then to wonder what was going on about Justin. Whenever he heard footsteps in the hall he peeked out to see who it was and where they were going. During the afternoon Mom went back and forth between the kitchen and Dad's study and Courtney went back and forth between the TV and the telephone. But Justin only came out of his room once all afternoon and that was just to go down the hall to the bathroom.

It was turning into a strange day. On the one hand, Matt had an uncomfortable premonition that something really bad was about to happen, but on the other hand, he didn't know why he thought so. There hadn't been any clues except for Justin missing church, which could just have been because he wasn't feeling well.

When Matt got to the dinner table that evening the first thing he noticed was that when he said hi to Justin, all he got was a dirty look. That wasn't much of a clue, however, because Justin stopped speaking to him pretty often these days. The only thing that made a difference this time was that Matt usually knew why, or at least could make a pretty good guess. This time he hadn't a clue.

He was still trying to remember what he might have done when he began to realize he wasn't the only one Justin wasn't speaking to. All during that Sunday dinner Justin said absolutely nothing to anyone, except when someone asked him if he wanted some more of something, and then he only shook his head, made a grunting noise and went on glaring at his plate. That was when Matt knew for certain that something seriously peculiar was going on. There was nothing the least bit normal about Justin turning down seconds.

When it was time for family sharing, Justin went on glaring at his plate while Dad called on Matt first and then Courtney. Matt told about how he'd gone to the library and read up on the history of Timber City, and Courtney told about her two new best friends, and which one she liked better than the other one, and why.

All the time Courtney was talking, and even while he was talking himself, Matt had been worrying about what might happen when it was Justin's turn. But it turned out to be worse than anything he'd imagined. When Dad started to say, "And now, son, in spite of the dark mood you seem to be in . . ." Justin jumped up so fast his chair slammed over backward, and without picking it up or saying a word, he stomped out of the room.

The rest of the family finished their dessert, but Courtney kept rolling her eyes and sighing dramatically. Matt was shocked and very curious. But when he tried to ask Dad what was wrong, Dad would only say that he and Mom had made a decision that Justin didn't agree with. But later Matt found out more by talking to Courtney.

"Oh, it was really a horrendous scene," she said, grabbing Matt and pulling him into her room. After she'd closed the door behind him, she said, "It was about Justin's friend, Lance. Do you know who Lance is?"

"Yeah, I know who he is. He's the one with the eyebrow ring and the spiky hair."

Courtney nodded. "Well, I guess somebody told Dad about some trouble that Lance has been in lately. And so Mom and Dad told Justin he couldn't ride around in Lance's truck anymore."

Matt didn't even know that Justin had been hanging

out with Lance. So he asked, "Where has he been going in Lance's truck?"

"Mostly around town, I guess," Courtney said, "but next weekend there's going to be this big beach blast and Justin was planning to go to the coast with Lance. And when Dad said he couldn't because the coast road was too dangerous, there was the most horrible scene."

She went on then to tell how she had listened to the whole thing from just outside the door of Dad's office and she'd heard every word. And she remembered every word too, and repeated all of them for Matt, with so many dramatic special effects and word-for-word quotations that Matt wound up feeling he'd been there too, right outside the office door.

"And then Dad went," Courtney said, " 'I know you're feeling disappointed now, but someday you'll realize . . .' And then Justin went, 'Someday? Like when I'm too old to give a damn. . . .' "

Matt winced. "Justin said *damn* to Dad?" he asked. Ordinarily Gerald Hamilton wasn't the kind of father a kid would say *damn* to.

Courtney nodded. "And a lot of worse words. And when Dad told him he was grounded he went, 'All right, I'll go to my room, but I won't stay there. And the next time Lance asks me to go with him, I'm going and you can't stop me.' "

Matt could hardly believe it. Nobody talked to Dad that way. And as if that weren't bad enough, Courtney went on to quote a bunch of stuff from the argument Mom and Dad had afterward because Mom thought Dad had been too easy on Justin.

"Mom went, 'You've always let Justin get away with behavior that you condemn in other people's children.' And Dad went, 'That's not fair, you know that's not fair.' And then Mom went . . . And Dad went . . ." And on and on and on.

"It was a horrendous argument." Courtney's voice was getting more high-pitched and dramatic with every quote. "I'm so frightened, Matt. I'm sure Mom and Dad are going to get divorced and Justin will get sent to juvenile hall, and who knows what will happen to you and me." She had been walking around the room as she talked, twisting her face into tragic mask expressions—expressions that she stopped to check on every time she went past a mirror. After the third or fourth trip around the room she threw herself down on her bed and buried her face in her pillow.

Matt didn't know what to do, so for a while he didn't do anything. He tried to remind himself that Courtney had a special talent for tragic drama, but he had to admit he'd never seen, or heard, anything quite like what she was doing at the moment. With her face buried in the pillow and her shoulders shaking violently, she was making a noise that sounded something like a howling coyote. A weird, muffled, quavering sound that rose and fell and rose again.

What could he do? Matt stood beside Courtney's bed for quite a while feeling hopeless and pretty helpless, before he suddenly had an idea. He sat down on the edge of the bed and started reciting one of the poems they'd made up when they used to play with Courtney's animal collection. The game they used to call the Breath of Life.

In a high-pitched singsong he chanted, "Open your eyes and breathe deep, wake from your enchanted sleep."

The howling faded away. Courtney turned over slowly and began to say, "Stamp your hoof and . . . See. I've forgotten what comes next." She sighed and the tragic quaver was back in her voice as she went on, "That proves it. Forgetting our poems just proves our happy childhood is all over. At least mine is."

"Oh come on. You remember." Matt tried to sound enthusiastic. "The next line was—'Stamp your hooves and shake your head.' Don't you remember? You always were the one who did the unicorn poem."

"Oh yes, I do remember now." Getting up off the bed, Courtney went to the high shelf, took down the spun-glass unicorn, breathed on its head three times and began to whisper, "Open your eyes and . . ."

Matt thought it might be a good time to leave. Getting up, he walked quietly to the door. With his hand on the knob, he turned back and said, "Courtney." He was sorry to interrupt the unicorn poem, but he had to know. "Courtney. How did you make that howling noise?"

Still holding the unicorn against her lips, Courtney said, "What howling noise? When?"

"Just now, while you were lying there with your face in the pillow."

"I wasn't making any noise," she said. "How could I howl with my face in the pillow?" Her eyes narrowed thoughtfully. "Yeah, I remember. I heard something too. I thought you were doing it. Wasn't it you?"

Matt shook his head slowly and firmly and, together, they walked across the room to the window. Standing side by side, they stared out past the big oak tree and the picket fence to the beginning of the forest. The sun was almost down and long shadows stretched out across the lawn. Long empty shadows.

"It sounded like a dog," Courtney said.

Matt felt a shiver run up the back of his neck. "A dog?" he said. "Yeah, I guess that is what it sounded like."

The shadows grew longer. A squirrel ran down one side of the oak tree and back up the other. Nothing else happened. Matt went back to his room.

Fifteen

Fifteen

A huge, almost full moon climbed slowly across the sky, turning the lawn to silver and the trees to black velvet silhouettes. On that particular night Matt spent a lot of time keeping track of the moon's slow, stately progress because dreams kept waking him up. Nightmares actually, one after another.

The first nightmare was about being lost in what seemed to be the basement of the Palace or else the lair of some enormous underground monster. Amelia was in the dream and Matt was desperately trying to follow her, but she wouldn't wait for him. She kept getting farther and farther away and Matt kept stumbling over what seemed to be the bodies of animals. Cold, clammy bodies, covered with bristly fur, that felt and smelled dead, except that some of them squirmed and squealed when he touched them.

Something was following him. A huge, shapeless blob was getting closer and closer, reaching out to wrap him in long, smothering tentacles. Something wound around his throat and he woke with a start, only to find that the strangling tentacle was the tangled bedsheet and the whole underground horror story had been only a dream.

And as if that weren't bad enough, an entirely different nightmare was waiting for him when he finally got back to sleep. This time he was in a courtroom with a judge and jury. There were chains on his hands and feet and the judge was shaking his finger and saying that Matthew Hamilton was guilty of having divorced parents and a brother who was in juvenile hall. Matt was crying and trying to tell the jury that it wasn't his fault because he hadn't meant to do it.

One of the jurors seemed to be a dog, a shaggy dog with sad, brown eyes. Matt could tell that the dog wanted to forgive him, but when it tried to say "not guilty," the other jurors hit and kicked it until it ran away yelping. Then the judge dragged Matt out of the courtroom and threw him into a tiny, dark room. His arms were flailing, pounding on the walls of the cell—when he woke up.

He was awake then, but even with both eyes wide open the nightmare hangovers kept flickering through his mind, until at last he got out of bed and went to the window.

Outside in the fading moonlight, nothing moved. The oak tree's black velvet leaves hung still and silent, and pale shadows lay limply on the silvery lawn. And beyond the yard the tall, slender pine trees marched away, rank after rank after rank. . . .

Marching ranks—like an endless file of soldiers. Alexander's soldiers advancing on the Persian army, or maybe the Greeks. Slipping down off the window seat, Matt lifted the lid, dug out a helmet and, a little farther down, a shield. A helmet and shield he'd made himself out of cardboard and glued-on Velcro and decorated with authentic designs he'd copied from the *M* volume of the encyclopedia. *M* for Macedonia.

Slapping the helmet on his head, he dug deeper, looking for the sword, but he couldn't find it in the dim light. Where was his Alexander the Great scimitar? He hadn't used it lately, but it had to be there somewhere—if only it hadn't been so dark.

He was on the way back from turning on the light when he happened to catch a glimpse of himself in the mirror. A glimpse of Matthew Hamilton, in plaid pajamas, with a pointed helmet on his head and a slightly bent shield strapped to his left arm. He stared for a moment, grinned ruefully and went back to dump the shield and helmet in the window seat. Not this time, he told himself. This time being Alexander the Great wouldn't solve anything. Not Alexander, or Robin Hood, or even Napoleon.

Half an hour later he was still on the window seat, wide awake and being tormented by nightmare reruns, when suddenly he tensed, focusing his eyes on . . . What was it that had moved out there on the lawn? He was sure he'd seen something, some small, shaggy animal, come out of the forest for a moment. Only for a moment and then, just as quickly, fade back out of sight.

Although he went on staring until his eyes felt dry and stiff, nothing else moved in the shadows at the edge of the trees. After a while he was forced to blink, and then blink again, and at last to let his eyes slowly close. Not to sleep but only to rest them for a moment, only for a moment, but that was when he heard a soft, comforting grumbling, like the sound Shadow used to make when he knew Matt was feeling bad.

With the friendly growl still echoing in his ears, Matt found his way back to bed and slid into a calm, comforting sleep. And sure enough, the next morning things did seem to be moving in a slightly better direction.

At breakfast Justin managed a mumbled "Okay" when Mom asked him if he wanted more pancakes, and Courtney had stopped acting like the leading lady in a Greek tragedy. And when Matt asked Dad if he could go for a long ride on his bike all Dad said was "Ask your mother," which was no surprise. But Mom's answer, "All right, all right. Run along," definitely was.

It all happened so much more quickly than he thought it would that it wasn't until he was on his way, pedaling toward Rathburn Park, that Matt realized he needed to make some plans. Plans like where he would look for Amelia and what he would do if he found her. The plans hadn't progressed very far when he turned into the park, got off his bike near the No Trespassing sign and found himself staring at—a famous person. Well, famous in Timber City at least.

The parking area was just about empty, which was normal for a weekday during working hours, but a car was pulling to a stop on the other side of the lot. A jeep actually, a beat-up, rusty old jeep. And as Matt watched, the door opened and this stranger, who somehow looked vaguely familiar, got out. Matt stared at the tall, red-haired man for a minute or two and then, suddenly, he knew. It was Red Sinclair.

Matt had never met Mr. Sinclair before, but he'd heard about him and he'd seen his picture at the top of his column in *The Timber City Morning Star*. He'd even read his whole column a couple of times when it was about something particularly interesting like whale watching or buried treasure. The Red Sinclair column was usually about local people and places and it often mentioned the ancient jeep the writer drove when he went out in the country looking for good story material. So when Matt saw a red-haired man with a big chin getting out of a rusty old jeep, it didn't take him very long to figure out who it had to be.

Under ordinary circumstances, Matt might have pedaled right over to say hello. He usually wasn't all that shy around adults, not even fairly famous ones. And it wasn't every day that he got to meet a column writer whose picture was in the local newspaper several times a week. But for some reason, maybe because he had been about to do something illegal, like disobeying a No Trespassing sign, he didn't make the first move. He was starting to get back on his bike when Mr. Sinclair waved and called to him.

"Hey, kid," he yelled, and then, "Are you Patrick?"

Matt walked his bike closer. "No," he said. "My name's Matthew Hamilton. I know who you are, though. I read your column."

"You do? Good for you. Glad to meet you, Matthew Hamilton." Red Sinclair shook Matt's hand. "Even if you aren't Patrick."

Red Sinclair reached into his jeep for some photographer's

stuff before he went on. "Somebody named Patrick e-mailed me yesterday about—well, something he'd seen in the park last weekend. Sounded like an interesting story, so I thought I might check it out."

"Here in Rathburn Park?" Matt asked.

Sinclair nodded. "Yep. Said he'd seen a ghost. And that he wasn't the only one who saw it. Said he was with some friends and they all saw the same thing."

Matt was very interested. "What did it look like?" he blurted out. "It wasn't a dog, was it?"

Mr. Sinclair stopped adjusting his camera and grinned at Matt. "A ghost dog?" he asked. "That's a new angle. Have you heard something about a ghost dog?"

Matt shook his head. "No, it just occurred to me. I mean, to wonder if there were dog ghosts. Do you think there are?"

Mr. Sinclair laughed. "Now, that's a question I've never been asked before. But now that you come to mention it, I don't see why it couldn't happen. I've known some pretty supernatural canine citizens in my day. But in this case it definitely wasn't a dog. According to my e-mail informant, it was a woman, or perhaps a girl. A girl dressed in a long white dress and wearing a hat with a heavy veil. He said he and his friends tried to follow her, but she ran away through the forest and then right out across the swamp and got away."

Some kind of mental volcano in the back of Matt's brain began erupting, spewing out a bunch of startling ideas. For a moment he was speechless, except for a silent voice inside his head that kept asking questions he didn't dare ask out loud. A girl? In a big floppy hat with lots of ribbons and velvet flowers?

The newspaper columnist finished getting all kinds of equipment slung over his shoulders and stuffed into the pockets of his safari vest and cargo pants before he interrupted Matt's train of thought. "Let's see," he said, pointing to the east. "The graveyard is over this way, isn't it?"

"The graveyard? Yes. Over there." Matt shook his head to clear away visions of a veiled and beribboned hat. "It's over this way." Pushing his bike, he led the way toward the graveyard. "Is that where the ghost was?"

"No. At least I'm not sure. The e-mail just said it was near the park. I probably wouldn't have paid much attention except an old-timer friend of mine told me a similar story very recently. Told me he'd come out to put flowers on some graves and he saw a girl in a long dress."

"Wow," Matt said. "Your friend saw a girl in a long white dress in the graveyard?"

"Well, actually in this case my informant described it as blue. A pale, lacy blue. The dress, that is. But long, ankle-length, and he did mention a big hat and a veil. Sounded similar. That's why I bit on this one. Two sources are always better than one. Don't you agree, Mr. Hamilton?"

"Oh yes," Matt said. "Two sources are better for historians, too." He went on to say that he was planning to be a writer of history books. Red Sinclair seemed interested, but just as Matt was about to mention some of the historical periods he was especially interested in, Mr. Sinclair said he thought they ought to stop talking so as not to scare off the ghost if she happened to be near-by, and Matt had to agree that was probably a good idea.

For a while Matt only watched from just outside the fence while Mr. Sinclair tramped around looking at grave-stones and taking notes. Matt couldn't help being impressed. With all that camera equipment hanging around his neck and bulging the pockets of his safari vest, Red Sinclair certainly looked like a famous newspaper reporter. When he came back and sat down on the rail fence, Matt joined him, and for several minutes they just sat there quietly waiting—and wondering. Waiting to see if the ghost was going to show up and wondering—at least Matt was wondering—about a girl ghost who wore a big hat with a veil.

He was also wondering how he could ask Mr. Sinclair some important questions without giving away a lot of secrets. Amelia's secrets mostly, but some personal ones too. Questions that would require some embarrassing explanations, like, for instance, how he, Matthew Hamilton, happened to meet a girl in a big floppy hat with a veil, inside a ruined church on strictly "No Trespassing" private property.

After they'd been quiet for a while without anything happening, Mr. Sinclair said he'd have to go, but he gave Matt his card and said to keep in touch. "And if you meet up with anything ghostly, either human or canine, please let me know."

Matt said he would.

Sixteen

Sixteen

After he watched Red Sinclair's old jeep disappear down the road, Matt pushed his bike back to the No Trespassing sign. There, at the beginning of the trail to the ruined church, he paused long enough to look around one more time just to be sure no one was watching. Nobody was. The coast was clear. Now that the jeep was gone, there was not a single car in the parking lot.

No one around. Not a living soul. Something about the not a *living soul* idea made a small shiver sneak up the back of his neck. He didn't exactly know why. Having the whole park to himself was actually a lucky break. A little bit lonely, maybe, and even kind of unnatural, but lucky in that there wouldn't be anyone around to point out the No Trespassing sign and mention that the ruins were on private property. Matt shivered again before he checked out the whole area one last time and pushed his bike around the No Trespassing sign and on down the narrow, overgrown path that led to the church.

Under the broken arch of the narthex he stopped again to park and lock his bike, and then to look and listen, to peer into the vine-draped jungle that filled the huge, roof-less room, and to listen to that special breathless silence he'd noticed before in historic places, particularly deserted ones. A silence that was like the people who had passed that way long ago were holding their breath as they listened and watched. Thinking about all those invisible watchers was pretty interesting. Matt shivered. Under the circumstances, almost too interesting. Backing quickly out of the entryway, he ducked into Amelia's secret pathway, which led around to the side entrance.

Arriving at the smaller entryway, Matt again peered into the large, roofless enclosure that had once been the main part of the church. From there, just as he remembered, one slanted wall of Old Tom's cabin was in plain view, and not that far away.

Matt couldn't help being tempted. On the one hand, he was sure he remembered how to get to the cabin door safely, by staying back against the church wall until he was almost there, to avoid the booby trap. On the other hand, he'd promised Amelia that he wouldn't go into the cabin by himself. And besides the promise, there was the danger, according to Amelia, that the ghost of Old Tom would get him if he did.

With his back pressed against the stone wall, Matt went over what Amelia had said on the subject exactly as he remembered it, word for word. "Old Tom's ghost would get you for sure if you came here by yourself," she'd said. But of course Matt hadn't believed it, at least not after he'd had a chance to think about it. To think and wonder why a ghost would bother to "get" a particular person and leave someone else alone. The whole thing, he decided, was pretty hard to swallow, particularly for a person who didn't believe in ghosts to begin with.

So what was he going to do right now, right at this very moment? The thing was—for some strange reason he really wanted to see the cabin again. He didn't know why or what he expected to find there. Amelia maybe? Amelia herself, sitting in Old Tom's broken rocking chair. He could picture her clearly, sitting in the chair and rocking slowly back and forth. Amelia in a long white dress and a big floppy hat . . .

Suddenly, impulsively, Matt leaned forward and called her name. Called, softly at first, and then just a little more loudly. "Amelia. Are you in there?" No answer. No answer except maybe a deepening of the breathless silence. So he tried again, but still not very loudly. Somehow it didn't seem right, or even possible, to shout in a church. Even a deserted one. Or maybe, especially in a deserted one.

He waited a while before he called one last time. Taking a deep breath, he cupped his hands around his mouth and called, but this time, not for Amelia. This time, without even deciding to, he opened his mouth and what came out was "Rover."

"Rover." The word echoed once, twice, faded away, and once again the listening silence deepened. Deepened, and lengthened until another sound seeped through. A faint murmur, or maybe a whimper, so slight and unreal that Matt wondered if it had come from his own throat.

He didn't try it again. Instead, he ducked into the bushy tunnel and scurried back to the main entrance—and his bicycle. Opening the bike's canvas pannier, he took out a pencil and notebook, thought for a minute and then began to write.

> *Hi, Amelia. It's Monday morning around eleven o'clock. I have to go home now, but I'll try to be back tomorrow or maybe Wednesday around nine-thirty. Okay?*
> *Matt*
> *P.S. I didn't go into the cabin.*

The next problem was where to leave the note. It had to be someplace where the wind wouldn't blow it away and yet where Amelia would be likely to see it. Looking around the narthex, Matt found plenty of nooks and crannies where one could hide a note. But in this case, a hiding place wasn't what he had in mind. The piece of paper needed to be where Amelia couldn't possibly miss it.

Giving up on the narthex, Matt made his way back through the tunnel path to the side door, and then suddenly, thinking only about a place to leave the note, he began to inch his way on into the church itself.

He didn't do it on purpose. It was more like he was following somebody, or something, that was leading the way. Holding the carefully folded note out in front of him, like a not-too-welcome guest at a fancy party might hold out his invitation, he sidled along the wall, skirted the crumbling edge of the booby trap pit, pushed open the cabin door on its rusty, creaking hinges and then there he was, inside the cabin—all by himself. Just where he'd promised he wouldn't be. Inside the rough wooden walls and under the sagging roof where Old Tom had lived and died, and where his dog, Rover, had returned night after night to wait and watch for his dead master to return.

Matt's throat thickened and his eyes began to burn as he looked at the rusty iron cot, the rickety old table, the broken rocking chair and the metal-banded trunk. Then he turned back again to stare at the cot until what he was actually seeing blurred into a scene in which a small, shaggy dog sat with his chin resting on the edge of an empty bed. Matt shook his head, blinked, and Mrs. McDougall's painting faded away. He swallowed hard and shook his head again, forcing his mind back to the problem of the moment—the problem of where to leave the note.

He was still trying to decide where Amelia would be certain to see it when his eyes happened to light on—the trunk. A nice flat surface, safely out of the wind, and very noticeable. He could leave the note right there, on top of Old Tom's trunk.

The note was in place, one edge of the paper tucked under a metal band, and Matt was getting to his feet when he noticed the bone. A large, old bone, chewed clean and dry, was lying right beside the iron cot. Surely he would have seen it when he was there before—if it had been there before.

Picking up the bone, Matt was examining it carefully, turning it back and forth in his hands, when he began to hear a faint whimpering murmur. Maybe a baby bird's call, but maybe not. He froze, motionless, except for turning his head from side to side to catch even the faintest rustle.

What was it? The sound came again, faint and

pleading. Matt was about to say, "It's all right. I won't take it," when the whimper suddenly became a yelp, followed closely by a noise of an entirely different nature. This sound was loud and definite, a metallic clatter followed by a heavy thud.

Dropping the bone and jumping to his feet, Matt hurried out of the cabin, out of the church and onto the tunnel path, where he ran, stooping and dodging, back to where his bicycle was . . . gone!

Well, not entirely gone. The bike was there, but it wasn't leaning against the narthex wall where he definitely had left it. A few feet down the trail, the bike was lying on its side. A bunch of pens and paper had spilled out of the pannier, there was a new dent in the hind fender and the front wheel was still slowly spinning.

Seventeen

Seventeen

There was a lot to think about. A lot of puzzling questions to be asked and answered, but not right away. At least not until he'd opened the lock, turning the dial with shaky fingers, put it away in the pannier, pushed the bike down the trail to the parking lot, jumped on and headed for home. And no answers even then, at least not while his mind was still busy warning him to watch for stop signs and lumber trucks and, at the same time, reminding him over and over again that he was seriously late.

Even after he was safely home, it was quite a while before he was able to arrive at any useful explanations of what had happened at the ruined church. The problem was that, from the moment he walked into his own house, there was too much other stuff to be considered. Stuff like whether Justin was still determined to go to the coast with Lance on Saturday night even if he didn't have permission. And whether Courtney was still in mourning because the Hamilton family was about to self-destruct.

Matt was home, establishing an alibi by standing

around outside on the back porch. Standing around long enough so he could say, "Oh, I've been home for quite a while," if anybody mentioned how late he was. He was still on the back porch when he began hearing voices.

The voices were Dad's and Justin's, and the subject was . . . Matt crept silently across the porch to the kitchen door. Right at first it was hard to catch the exact words, but the general tone was pretty easy to interpret. Dad and Justin were definitely having a really serious argument. But then, loud and clear, Justin said, "Yeah, I hear you, Dad. But the thing is, that's a lie. All of it. Who told you that stuff?"

Frozen in his tracks, Matt couldn't help listening—and trying to figure out whether things were getting better or worse. Worse, judging by the anger in Justin's voice. Or maybe better? At least he was talking instead of refusing to say anything to anybody.

Putting his ear to the edge of the door, Matt heard Dad's answer. "Some people told your mother originally and then—"

"Oh sure," Justin interrupted. "Those club ladies, I bet. All those old women who hate people like Lance just because he doesn't . . ." Justin hushed then as if he'd guessed someone was listening, so Matt scooted back to bang the door and walk noisily across the back porch. When he came into the kitchen Justin was on his way out of the room and he didn't stop or look back when Matt said, "Oh, hi, Justin."

Dad was standing by the sink with a glass of water in his hand. He smiled at Matt in a distant, disconnected way and went on looking toward where Justin had disappeared.

After a minute or two, Matt went on through the kitchen toward the sound of another conversation.

This time the voices were Mom's and Courtney's, and they went right on talking when Matt came into the living room. The first thing Matt noticed was that Courtney had definitely stopped doing the Greek tragedy bit. Actually, Matt decided after checking her out again, she seemed to have changed the wailing mask for the grinning one.

"Well, we mustn't get our hopes up." Mom didn't sound quite as overjoyed. "We've tried other treatment programs before without much success and . . ." She stopped when she saw Matt. "Matthew! Where on earth have you been? I've been worrying about you."

"Oh, hi," Matt said, so busy wondering if someone had come up with a cure for whatever was ailing Justin, he even forgot to use the "Oh, I've been home for quite a while" alibi. Instead, he only said, "What kind of treatment?"

"For allergies." Courtney's smile was cover-girl bright and shiny. "For my allergies."

"Oh. Oh sure, your allergies." He tried not to grin. He knew Courtney's allergies weren't funny, but he couldn't help being pleased that, at the moment, the new allergy treatment seemed to have taken Mom's mind off the time of day. The definitely-too-late time of day.

It wasn't until evening when he was alone in his own room that Matt was able to get down to making sense of it all. Or at least start trying to. To make some sense out of what was going on in Rathburn Park as well as right there in the Hamilton family.

Sitting in his favorite spot on the window seat, he looked out at the twisted oak tree and the smooth sweep of lawn and waited for the soft, green silence to make his mind stop jittering from one thing to another and get down to business.

First of all, there was Red Sinclair's ghost story to think about. A story about a ghostly girl wearing a long, old-fashioned dress and a big hat with a veil who had been haunting the graveyard and Rathburn Park.

Closing his eyes, he could bring back sharply and cleanly his first meeting with Amelia, when she had suddenly appeared behind him, dressed in a frilly, old-fashioned blouse and skirt and *a big, floppy hat tied on with a veil.* It was that memory that brought with it the alarming possibility that what Red Sinclair's informants had actually seen was—Amelia. And even more disturbing, if they had seen Amelia, did it mean they only *thought* they'd seen a ghost? Or—and this was the weirdest possibility—could it mean that Amelia really was what they thought she was? It was a thought that made a strange tingle crawl up Matt's backbone and right on up the back of his head.

He shook his head hard, thinking that was just plain crazy. Amelia couldn't be a ghost. Not that he, Matt Hamilton, was any kind of authority on the subject, but everything he'd ever read or heard about ghosts made it clear that they tended to be pretty flimsy, unsubstantial characters. Like you could walk right through one and not feel a thing, except maybe a kind of hair-raising chill. Bringing to mind how Amelia had jerked him around by the back of his shirt, Matt knew for sure that, ghost or not, there wasn't anything flimsy about Amelia.

But that still left some other mysteries, like what had happened to the bicycle, for instance. In the few minutes it had taken him to run around the church and leave the note in Old Tom's cabin, someone not too unsubstantial had managed to throw the locked bicycle two or three yards away from where he'd left it.

And then there was the Dolly question. The only thing Matt knew for certain about Dolly was that he was positive he had heard someone in the Palace calling her name. And when he'd asked Amelia about her, she had said, "Dolly is just a ghost."

So if there was a ghost and her name was Dolly, where did she come from, and how did Amelia happen to know about her?

And then there was the bone. A clean-looking, frayed-at-the-edges bone that looked like . . . Well, what it definitely reminded Matt of was an old ham bone that Shadow used to carry around Mrs. McDougall's backyard. A bone that looked like it had been chewed on for a long time. But the important questions for Matt were how long it had been lying there beside Old Tom's cot, and why he hadn't noticed it before.

The questions, all of them, kept parading through Matt's mind, one after the other, and then as it got later and he got sleepier, began mixing together in a senseless jumble.

It was quite late when he woke up in the middle of a nightmare to find he'd forgotten to go to bed. Curled up in an uncomfortable position on the window seat, he woke up to find that his right arm had gone to sleep and his head was full of scenes from a nightmare. A vivid, Technicolor nightmare in which a purple pickup truck was stopping in front of the house and Justin was going out and climbing into it. Mom and Dad had been in the dream too, standing in the front yard in their pajamas shouting at Justin to come back. And as the truck drove away with Justin in it, Matt could see that there wasn't anyone behind the wheel. The truck was driving itself.

Eighteen

Eighteen

On Wednesday Matt's bike ride to Rathburn Park once again wasn't hard to arrange. Mom had taken Courtney to see the new allergy doctor, Dad was having a meeting that would probably last most of the day, and right after Dad left, Justin disappeared too. Matt didn't see him leave, but he hoped it hadn't been in a purple pickup.

It was a hot July day. Almost as hot as summer in Six Palms. But as Matt pedaled toward the park, his mind wasn't on the weather. Instead it kept doing a mental rerun of the part of the nightmare where Justin climbed into the cab of the truck and roared away into the night with nobody behind the wheel. But as soon as he turned in at the park, the pickup truck nightmare began to fade. As he parked and locked his bike in the narthex of the old church other worries began to take over. Living, wide-awake nightmares, for instance, like the one that brought to mind the P.S. he'd added to his note to Amelia. The one he'd jotted down in a hurry to say he hadn't been inside Old Tom's cabin. And which he'd wound up leaving right there *in the cabin* on top of the old trunk. How was he going to explain that?

Feeling almost shriveled with embarrassment, Matt pictured himself trying to make Amelia understand how it had happened. "Well," he imagined himself saying, "when I wrote the note, I hadn't gone inside yet and I wasn't planning to, but then I couldn't find a good place to leave the note where you'd be sure to find it and so I kind of . . ."

He couldn't help wondering how far he'd be able to get with that explanation before Amelia would quit listening and start throwing punches. He was wincing, wondering where she'd hit him, when he began to hear something that turned embarrassment into fear. What he suddenly heard was a deep, raspy voice that seemed to be coming from—only a few feet away. Filtering out from among the tangle of vine-draped saplings in the nave of the church, it was saying, "All right, you stupid kid. Now you're going to get it."

Matt was terrified. But even as he backed away, dragging his bicycle, stumbling over it and going down on one knee, he began to notice some changes in the weird voice. Some raspy squeaks that were beginning to make it sound more like the voice of—a kid. Maybe even the voice of a female kid.

He had dropped the bike and was inching his way back down the trail when suddenly an absolutely amazing apparition appeared in the entryway. Framed in the archway, a short, bulky figure was stomping its feet and waving its arms in a threatening manner. Not tall, but broad-shouldered and thick-chested, the strange creature was dressed in a long dusty black coat and a tall black hat.

There wasn't much face showing below the hat, but what little there was was black too. At least streaked and smeared with black. Matt's gasp at the suddenness of its appearance quickly turned into a snort of laughter.

"All right, Amelia," he managed to say. "You can knock it off. I know it's you."

It was Amelia, all right, dressed in a huge black coat and a stovepipe hat, both of which looked like something from another century. For a moment longer she went on waving her arms and making strange noises, while Matt went on trying not to laugh. Finally she jerked the hat off her head and threw it down fiercely, and began to struggle out of the coat, while strands of hair straggled down around her ears and sooty rivers of sweat trickled down her blackened face.

"Hot," she was muttering. *"Hot.* I'm dying."

Matt watched in amazement while the coat was followed by several other layers of clothing, all of which seemed to be stuffed full of padding of various sorts. What seemed to be the ragged remains of towels and shawls and shirts and sweaters piled up around her, until she was finally down to a sleeveless white cotton shirt that hung to her knees. Wiping her face with both hands before she put them on her hips, she gave Matt a dangerous, three-alarm glare.

Matt stepped quickly back out of reach before he struggled to erase his grin and started to ask, "What—why—" Then he settled for "Where in the world did you get all that stuff?" He stooped to pick up the tall hat. Turning it from side to side and gently dusting it off, he said, "Wow. I'll bet this hat is a hundred years old at least."

Amelia breathed heavily a few more times before her

frown began to relax. "Yeah, I know," she said. "The attic is full of stuff like that."

"Really?" Matt said. Thinking about the kinds of things you might find in the attic of an ancient place like the Palace was pretty exciting. It wasn't hard to imagine what it would be like to explore a huge room packed full of all that antique stuff, and the imagining was making him forget to worry about what Amelia might do next. Picking up the coat, he examined it carefully, running his fingers over the high collar, the braided trim and the soft satiny lining. "Wow," he said again. "May I try it on?"

Amelia shrugged angrily and the sizzle between her teeth gradually became words. "Help yourself," she sizzled. "Go on. Put it on. The heat will kill you. I hope it does."

Matt put the coat on. It was hot, all right, and way too big. The man it had been made for must have had a huge barrel chest and long thick arms. "Doesn't exactly fit, does it?" he said.

"I know," she said. "That's why I had to have all that padding."

Matt took the coat off and folded it carefully while Amelia watched intently. When he'd finished folding he said, "Thanks," and smiled, but she only went on glaring. Feeling embarrassed, he turned away, and then glanced back—at her dirty face. "And that"—he gestured—"on your face?"

"It's charcoal," she said. Using the tail of her shirt, she wiped her face hard, rearranging the black smears a little but not getting rid of much of it. "I wanted to make a fake beard. I thought maybe I could find an old wig or something to make into a beard, but I couldn't find anything. So I drew it on with charcoal. It looked all right at first, but I probably sweated most of it off. I'll bet you wouldn't have recognized me if I'd been able to make a beard out of real hair."

Trying not to laugh, Matt nodded solemnly. "Maybe not," he said. Noticing that Amelia's frown was changing back to red alert, he edged away a little before he started to say, "Look, I'm sorry I—"

"Sorry," she practically shouted. "No you're not. Not sorry enough, anyway. Not enough for doing exactly what you promised you wouldn't do. And then writing a note that lied about it."

Matt nodded. "About the note," he said. "The note and the P.S." He waited a minute and then said it again. "About that P.S. If you'd just listen a minute, I could explain about the P.S."

"Oh yeah." Amelia's frown was fading again. "Okay, explain. This I got to hear."

So he did. It took a while to tell it all. How he'd given up on finding her and decided to leave a note, but then how, after he'd written it he couldn't find a good place to leave it, where it would be safe, but where she'd be sure to see it. "So I just went on into the cabin for a minute, just for a minute, to put it where you'd be sure to find it."

It seemed to be working. Amelia's face was unclenching a little. Still staring intently, she said, "Okay, okay. So you didn't stay very long."

"Right, not even a minute."

"And you didn't try to open the trunk?" Amelia was watching him closely, with narrowed eyes.

Puzzled, Matt shook his head. "No, why would I do that? I just left the note there."

She nodded thoughtfully for a moment before she said, "And what did you call me?"

He didn't know what she was talking about, at least not at first. "What did I call you? When? When did I call you something?"

"At the door of the church. The side door. Just before you left."

So she had been there after all. But where? Not in the cabin, he was sure of that. There just wasn't any hiding place inside the cabin where someone, even someone as small as Amelia, could be out of sight.

"So where were you?" he asked.

"Wouldn't you like to know? Maybe I was right there in the cabin only you couldn't see me. Maybe I can be invisible when I want to be."

For a moment he was almost ready to believe . . . But then he grinned. Invisible or not, she couldn't have been there in the cabin and then reached his bicycle before he did.

"Yeah. As if," he said. "And how about my bicycle? Didn't you move my bike?"

She grinned. Reaching out, she pretended to grab the handlebars of the bike. "Yeah. Want to see how I did it? I picked it up and threw it. Like this." Spinning around, she acted out throwing a heavy object down the trail.

Okay. So she'd heard him call and then she got to the front of the church before he did and . . . "Where were you—" he was starting to ask when she interrupted.

"Never mind where I was. But I heard you, all right. I heard you call Amelia, and then you called me another name."

126

He remembered then. "Oh," he said. "I wasn't calling you. Not then. I was calling—Rover." He shrugged, feeling a little embarrassed. "I don't know why exactly, but sometimes I wonder if Rover is still around."

Amelia looked puzzled. "Rover. Who's Rover?"

Matt stared in amazement. "You mean you don't know about Rover?"

She shook her head slowly. Her voice had a sarcastic tone as she said, "No, I don't know about Rover. So why don't you tell me?"

Matt thought for a moment before he said, "Well, okay, I will. I'll tell you about Rover—if you'll tell me about Dolly."

It took her a while to decide but finally, with her eyes still narrowed thoughtfully, she said, "Okay. I'll tell you, but you go first. Tell me about Rover."

"Okay," Matt said. "I will."

Nineteen

Nineteen

Matt was puzzled. Mrs. Keeler, the librarian, had said that everybody in town had known about Old Tom's dog, so it did seem that the Rathburns would have known about him too. Of course, Amelia, this particular Amelia, wasn't around when Old Tom was alive, but she'd heard about Old Tom, so someone in her family must have told her about him and how he'd lived in the church after the fire. So why not about Rover?

"About Rover," he began. "I wonder why your family didn't tell you about Rover."

"My family?"

"The Rathburns. They must have known about Rover."

Amelia shrugged. "Oh yeah, the Rathburns. Maybe they did know about him. But they didn't tell me. There's not that many Rathburns left, you know."

"I know," Matt said. Taking a deep breath, he paused, thinking about how to begin. "In fact, Mrs. Keeler told me—"

Amelia put her finger to her lips. "Hush," she said. "Listen." And then Matt heard it too. A car's motor and the crunch of tires on gravel. "Stay here. And be quiet." She disappeared down the trail that led to the parking lot, but in just a moment she was back. "Come on," she said. "We'd better go. It's a car full of people."

"Why do we have to go?" Matt said. "They're probably just going to the picnic grounds or the ballpark. They won't come in here, will they?"

"Maybe not," Amelia said. "But sometimes people come up the path a little way to get a look at the church. Kids mostly. Usually they get scared and go back before they get this far. But we better move just in case."

"All right," Matt said. "But my bicycle. What about my bike?" Amelia knew the answer to that, too. Pushing back a low-hanging tree limb, she quickly shoved the bike past a thick bush and into a cavelike cubbyhole in the underbrush.

"Hey, this is a neat hideout," Matt said, and then, wondering if this was where she'd been when he'd called to her and then to Rover, "Do you hide here sometimes?"

"Yeah, sometimes. But I've got lots of better hiding places than this one." Gathering up the stuff she'd used to pad the coat, she shoved it into Matt's arms. "Put this stuff with the bike," she said. "I'll be right back." She grabbed the old coat and hat and disappeared down her secret trail. After stashing the pile of padding in the underbrush, Matt returned to the narthex, and in a few minutes Amelia was back too.

"Okay," she whispered. "Let's get out of here." She led the way then, down another almost invisible path that angled away from the church and the parking lot. The trail twisted, turned, ducked under low-hanging branches and around huge, thorny blackberry barricades and finally stopped in a small clearing not far from the swamp. At the edge of the clearing the trunk of a fallen tree made a kind of bench. Scooting up onto the trunk, Amelia said, "Nobody ever comes here. It's too close to the swamp."

Matt was impressed. Amelia did seem to have all kinds of mysterious information, at least about the Rathburn forest. Like Robin Hood had known all the secret places in Sherwood. All the hidden trails and hideouts and—

"Okay." Amelia's sharp voice interrupted his thoughts. "Sit down and start talking. Tell me about this Rover person, and why you were calling him. What's the rest of his name, and what made you think he might be somewhere around here?"

Matt was grinning as he climbed up on the log. "Well," he began, "in the first place he is . . . I mean he *was* a dog. Mrs. Keeler at the library was the one who told me about him. He was Old Tom's dog."

"Old Tom's dog?" She was obviously surprised, and very interested. It didn't take Matt long to tell the whole story. How the dog named Rover had lived with Old Tom in the shack in the ruins of the church and how, when Tom died, the dog went on living there.

"He went on living right there in Old Tom's shack?" Amelia's eyes were wide and unblinking.

"He must have," Matt said. "Mrs. Keeler said there was a story going around that he slept on his master's grave, but when people went to look for him he was never there. He came into town every day and people would feed him, but he wouldn't stay with anybody. He lived to be very old for a dog, I guess, and when he finally died, the people who lived in Timber City in those days buried him beside his master. Mrs. Keeler said she was a little kid at the time but she could remember when that happened. And they even made him a gravestone. You know, that little stone tablet right beside Old Tom's grave. I think that must be the one."

"Oh yeah," Amelia murmured, as if talking to herself. "I wondered about that gravestone." A minute later she whispered, "Rover." After that she didn't say anything more for a long time and neither did Matt. Sitting side by side on the tree trunk, they were quiet for so long that when Amelia said, "Matt," suddenly and sharply, he jumped—and almost fell off the log. *"Matt,"* she said, and then, more quietly, "What else do you know about him? About Rover?"

Matt shook his head. "Not much," he was starting to say when, without even planning to, he began, "I think that after Old Tom died, Rover would just sit there on the floor of the cabin with his chin on the cot, like this . . ." Demonstrating, pretending to be a sad-eyed dog resting his chin on the edge of something, he felt his throat and eyes reacting like they always did when he thought about the picture in Mrs. McDougall's living room of the sad-eyed dog grieving for his dead master.

Amelia was watching with narrowed eyes. "How do you know he did that?" she said. "Did someone see him doing that?"

"Oh—oh well," Matt stammered, "not exactly. I just used to look at a picture like that. A picture . . ." And then Matt found himself not only telling Amelia about Mrs. McDougall and her dogs and the painting in her living room, but going right on to tell about the Fourth of July picnic and how the small shaggy dog had rescued him when he was lost in the woods. And how he'd had the feeling ever since that Rover was still around, kind of keeping an eye on things and maybe looking out for people he liked.

Amelia listened to the whole thing without saying a word, and without reacting at all, except that her dark eyes went wide and unblinking. When he finally ran out of things to tell, she took a long slow breath and said, "Yeah. I think I *did* know about Rover after all. I mean, nobody ever told me about him before, but . . ." She paused and then went on, "I just knew. I mean I've heard him barking and . . . and I think I've seen him, too, like you said." She was staring out toward the swamp with that faraway look in her eyes. "Yeah, I think I know about Rover."

Matt was puzzled. He wished he knew what to believe. What to believe about a lot of things. Like Rover—and Dolly. And Amelia herself. He really wished he knew just what to believe about Amelia.

Suddenly remembering the rest of the bargain they'd made, he said, "Well, okay, it's your turn now. It's your turn to tell me about Dolly."

As Amelia turned to face him, her eyes slowly lost the far horizon look and began to narrow. "All right," she said, "about Dolly. Dolly is . . . Well, she's a ghost too, like Rover. Only she's the ghost of a girl who used to live in the Palace a long time ago. Her real name was Amelia, like a lot of girls in the Rathburn family. Dolly was . . ." Another pause and then, "Dolly was just her nickname." She nodded. "Yeah, Dolly was the nickname of the Amelia that's in this big painting in the Palace." Amelia paused and, smiling that strange, out-of-focus smile, she stared off into the distance. At last she sighed and went on, "In the picture she's wearing this old-fashioned lacy dress with a high collar . . ." She paused again and her hand went to her throat. "With a gold locket around her neck, and a big hat and . . ." Suddenly she was watching Matt carefully as she repeated, "A big hat sort of tied on with a veil."

Matt was definitely wondering again. "But we did hear someone calling her," he said, "that day when you let me visit the Palace. Who was calling her?"

Amelia frowned. "Someone was calling Dolly? I don't remember hearing anything like that."

This time Matt was sure she was lying. Everything about that visit to the Palace was very clear in his memory. Everything, and particularly the voice calling Dolly.

"Well, I did," he said. "It went *'Dolly.'* It was loud and angry sounding. Not much like a ghost."

Amelia slid down off the tree trunk. "Oh yeah. How do you know what a ghost sounds like? Anyway, I've told you about Dolly and now I want to go see Rover's gravestone."

Twenty

I t was getting pretty late by the time they started to go to the graveyard so Amelia could look at Rover's grave. All the way there, taking a long and roundabout trail, Amelia was very quiet. "Hush" was all she would say when Matt tried to say something or ask a question. Pointing toward the ballpark, where they occasionally got a glimpse of a father giving his kids batting practice, Amelia would only shake her head and say, "Hush. You want them to hear us?"

Matt didn't think there was much danger, but he finally gave up trying to talk and followed Amelia silently along the winding pathway, over the graveyard's rail fence and into the neglected, overgrown corner where Old Tom was buried. On her knees beside the larger gravestone, Amelia eagerly pushed away a thick tangle of ivy until the small stone marker was exposed to the light.

"See," Matt said. "It's all mossy. You can't really tell what it used to say."

"I can," Amelia said, busily scratching away mud and moss with her fingernails. "It says 'Rover.' See!" She jerked on Matt's shirt, pulling him down toward the gravestone.

Matt shook his head. He didn't see it. At least not exactly. Maybe the vague squiggle was a part of an *R,* and maybe not.

"Rover," she repeated, "Rover." And then more loudly, almost calling, "Rover." Suddenly lifting her head, she tipped it from side to side as if she were listening, and then, turning to Matt, she said, "There, did you hear that? I did. I heard a dog barking."

Matt shook his head. "No," he said firmly. Very firmly. "I didn't. And neither did you." He was feeling angry without knowing why, until he realized what was going on and began to grin. It was pretty ridiculous to be jealous of a dog, particularly one that wasn't yours and wasn't even exactly real. To feel like Amelia should just stick to her own ghosts and keep her hands off other people's.

"Yes, I did," Amelia insisted. "Listen."

They'd both been listening for quite a while without hearing anything, at least Matt hadn't, when Amelia suddenly jumped up. Whispering, "Uh-oh. I forgot," she pulled at a chain that hung around her neck. A chain that held a small silver key and a large gold locket. A locket that opened to become a watch.

"Hey, I have to go," she said, staring at the watch face.

"Oh yeah. I do too." Matt moved closer, looking at the watch. "Hey, that's cool," he said. "It's very old, isn't it? My mom has one sort of like it that used be my grandmother's. Only it doesn't run anymore. And what's the key for?"

"This locket isn't my grandmother's," Amelia said. "It's mine." Her eyes narrowed. "And the key is none of your business." She put the watch and the key back under her shirt and then suddenly grabbed Matt by the front of his shirt. "Okay. Come on Friday next time. And in the meantime . . ." She shook a finger in his face. "Don't you go near the cabin. You hear me?"

Grinning as he peeled her fingers off his shirt, Matt said, "Okay. I won't. Not even to leave a note. And I'm not sure about Friday, but I think I can make it."

She was gone then, whirling and disappearing around a big bush. A moment later he caught another quick glimpse of her, farther away and still running, darting in and out between trees almost like some kind of . . . Like a bird or an animal, or maybe—a ghost?

He waited until she had disappeared entirely before he turned back for a last look at Rover's tombstone. Squatting down, he put one finger on the mossy scratches that might say . . . "Rover?" he whispered, and then, suddenly remembering, "Rover, how about that bone? Was that yours?"

Nothing. No sound except birds chirping and now and then a distant shout from the ballpark. A distant shout? Maybe a distant bark, or maybe not. And then nothing more. At least nothing he could be exactly sure of.

Sighing, he got up and started back toward the church and his bicycle. He ran at first, the way Amelia had done, skimming along the narrow trail and leaping over stumps and logs, but not for long. After he'd tripped jumping over a log and landed on his hands and knees he went back to walking, but fast, hurrying to get home as quickly as possible.

Home to a bunch of people who didn't seem to be speaking to each other or to Matt himself except to bawl him out for being late again and to tell him he was going to be grounded for the rest of the week. It was his mom who said, "That does it. You are grounded for one week. And don't try to argue, young man. You certainly had fair warning." So that was that. No arguing, no trying to explain and no more conversation.

The only exception to the general lack of conversation was Courtney, who was talking on the telephone. Talking excitedly, but not making much sense. Matt was on his way down the hall to his room when he passed Courtney going the other way, holding her cell phone to her ear. As they passed she was saying, "I know. Isn't it totally awesome, I mean, after all these years? I mean it feels like some kind of miracle." She listened again for a second and then gave an excited squeal. "Really, do you think I could? How old are they? Are you sure? I can't believe it's really going to happen."

She reached out then, grabbed Matt's arm and pulled him to a stop. "Stop, wait a minute," she said to Matt, and then, into the phone, "No, not you, Brittany. I was talking to my brother." She listened again and then giggled, "No, not the hunk. The little one. I want to tell him . . ."

He knew then who she was talking to. Brittany was one of her new best friends, but he had no idea what the rest of the excited conversation had been about, and he didn't much care. So when Courtney loosened her grip on the brother who wasn't a "hunk," he pulled away and went on down the hall.

It was only after he was in his own room that he began to realize just how bad everything was. At least for him. Grounded for a whole week. That meant he wouldn't be seeing Amelia. Not on Friday or the next day either. By the time he was free to get back to Rathburn Park there was no telling if he'd be able to find her, or if she'd speak to him if he did.

Grounded. Grounded in a house where everyone else was rushing around from place to place. The rest of that week Dad was gone as usual to his City Hall office and to all sorts of meetings, and Mom to her lunches and teas and club meetings, and Courtney to her new friends' houses. Justin was gone a lot too, but he never said where he was going. At least not where Matt could hear him.

Not that Matt was all alone in the house very often. Usually at least one member of the family was there temporarily on the way in or out. The only times everyone was there at once was at dinner, and even then no one did much talking, at least not the kind of talking that meant anything. And, in the case of Justin, not even that. Justin was still giving the whole family the silent treatment.

It was on Friday afternoon that Matt caught Dad just as he was going out the door for a meeting with the mayor, and managed to get in a request for a shortened sentence.

"You know, like paroled for good behavior? I haven't set one foot out of our yard since I got grounded, and I mowed the lawn once and took out the garbage twice. I think that's pretty good behavior, don't you?"

Dad grinned in a fairly sympathetic way and said he thought it was a possibility but there would have to be a meeting of the parole board before he could say for sure. Which obviously meant the same as "Ask your mother," which was usually bad news. Dad went on out to the car and Matt went out to sit on the front steps and stare down the road in the direction of Rathburn Park. He was still sitting there when a kid on a bicycle pedaled by and then came back and stopped.

"Hey," the kid yelled. "I know who you are. You must be one of the Hamiltons."

"Good guess," Matt said. "I don't know you, do I?"

It turned out the kid's name was Brett Hardacre. He was kind of ordinary-looking, with freckles and a shaggy haircut, and he really liked to talk. Which made for an easy conversation, because most of the time Matt only had to listen. He found out right away that he and Brett were almost the same age, and that Brett would also be starting his first year at the Timber City middle school in September.

Brett talked some about the elementary school he'd been going to in Timber City and how he felt about starting middle school. "I'm not too stoked about it, I guess," he said. "I mean, just when you get used to being one of the big kids, they make you start all over at the bottom of the heap."

"I know what you mean," Matt said. "Back to the bottom of the heap." He shrugged. "Oh well, I'm pretty used to it. Being the youngest one in my family and everything, I'm kind of—"

"Hey! What do you know? Me too," Brett interrupted. "It's the pits, isn't it? I got two of them. And both of them are boxers."

"Boxers?" Matt was confused. "You mean dogs? Boxer dogs?"

Brett laughed so hard he almost fell over his bicycle. "No. I mean prizefighters. I have two big brothers and they both take boxing lessons." Putting down his kickstand, he clenched his fists and started shadowboxing, jumping around and hitting the air with one fist and then the other. It looked to Matt like he knew what he was doing.

"So, how about you?" Matt asked. "Are you one too? A boxer, I mean?"

"Me?" Brett's laugh had an unhappy edge. "Not me. All I get to be is the punching bag."

Matt said he knew the feeling. They went on exchanging gripes for quite a while before Matt suddenly realized that Brett might know the answer to an important question.

"Hey, Brett," he said. "Did a girl who lives in the Palace go to your school last year? Her name is Amelia Rathburn."

"A girl named Amelia?" Brett shook his head, looking puzzled. "No. I don't think there are any kids living in the Palace. My grandmother said there's just this one old lady and a few other old people who work for her."

"Oh," Matt said. "Are you sure? Are you sure no kids live there?"

"Yeah, I'm sure. My grandmother has been there in person to talk to the old lady, and she never said anything about any kids. And I'm positive there wasn't anybody named Amelia at Lincoln Elementary. Not since I've been going there."

Matt was puzzled. "Well, if there were any kids living at the Palace where would they go to school? Are there other schools they might go to?"

Brett nodded. "Yeah, I suppose so. There's some other schools out in the new part of town, and a couple of private schools. But the thing is, I don't think there are any kids living at the Palace. If they were, my grandma would know about it. And talk about it." He grinned. "My grandma talks a lot."

Suddenly Matt made the connection. Hardacre. That

was the name of the woman who had permission to take people on tours of the Rathburn ruins on special occasions. The one who knew everything about the Rathburn family and the history of the town. So it looked like the woman who was practically a world-class authority on the Rathburn family was sure that the only Amelia living at the Palace was the one who was nearly one hundred years old.

After Brett pedaled off, Matt went on sitting on the front steps, wondering about a lot of things. Like, if he would ever see Amelia again. And, if he did see her, what would she be wearing? And would he have the nerve to ask her where she went to school, and if she didn't go, why not?

Twenty-one
Twenty-one

Matt got up on Saturday morning hoping to have a chance to ask his mom—the parole board—if he could get his grounding sentence revoked, or at least get some time off for good behavior.

He'd stayed awake for at least an hour the night before, getting his arguments lined up so he could present a convincing case. He'd felt pretty confident, but at the breakfast table the next morning it didn't go the way he had planned. To begin with, it was hard to get anybody's attention, or even to get a word in edgeways. Harder than usual, in fact. It took a while for Matt to figure out why.

The trouble was, as he soon began to realize, there were a lot of other petitions being presented that morning besides the one he wanted to talk about. Some of them were pretty up-front and undisguised, like Courtney's request to be allowed to go to Eureka for the weekend with Brittany and her family.

But there were some other things going on that were less up-front and a lot more complicated. Like what his parents were saying by chatting in a superrelaxed, not-a-worry-in-the-world way about how they were going to spend the day. Like the message was that they were sure that Justin hadn't meant it when he said he was going to the coast tonight with Lance whether they liked it or not.

And Justin was sending a message too, by acting unusually sociable and agreeable, finding something fairly polite to say to everyone, even Matt. And even going so far as to put his own dishes in the dishwasher, which was practically unheard of. The message obviously was that his parents had nothing to worry about, and it looked to Matt like Mom and Dad were falling for it.

But Matt himself wasn't so sure, having learned the hard way that his big brother was not above using his version of sweet talk to get a person right where he wanted him. So Matt listened to Justin chatting up the rest of the family, and went on wondering what Justin was really planning to do about Lance Layton and his purple pickup.

It wasn't very long before Dad had to rush out to a groundbreaking for Timber City's new police station and Mom left for an AAUW lunch, taking Courtney along to be dropped off at Brittany's house. So the parole board was gone, and Matt still hadn't gotten around to asking if he could be ungrounded. So there he was—home alone again except for Justin, who quickly disappeared into his room and slammed the door.

At first Matt really didn't have any definite plans. But by the time he'd finished reading the comics and watering the lawn, he'd made up his mind that the grounding sentence would certainly have been lifted if there'd been time to talk about it. The more he thought about it, the more sure he was that his parents would have agreed with him if they'd had time to listen to his argument. So after he'd eaten one of the tuna sandwiches Mom had left in the refrigerator, he got out his bike and headed toward Rathburn Park.

It was hot again, probably somewhere around ninety, which made bicycling as far as the park a pretty sweaty affair. The closer he got to the park's narrow valley, the hotter it seemed to get. The wooded hillsides were shutting out every bit of the west wind that usually brought with it a hint of cool ocean air.

At last, sweating and panting, Matt pedaled into the Rathburn parking lot and found there were only a couple of cars in the whole place; a red SUV and a pale gold sedan. And no one at all out on the ball field. That puzzled him for a minute. Usually the park was pretty busy on Saturdays. But then he figured out that anyone who usually came to the park on Saturday afternoons probably had headed for the coast instead to get out of the heat.

Lucky for them, and lucky for him, too, Matt thought, as he checked carefully in every direction before he ducked under the No Trespassing sign and pulled his bike around the barricade. A few minutes later, under the rough stone arch of the narthex, he stopped to lock his bicycle and peer briefly into the church itself.

Nothing moved in the tangled underbrush. Turning away, Matt pushed aside the fern fronds that camouflaged the entrance to Amelia's secret passageway, ducked into it and a moment later arrived at the side entrance.

Reminding himself sternly of his promise to Amelia, he only leaned in under the door frame, twisting his neck to look toward Old Tom's cabin. Inside the huge roofless room everything, leaves and needles and twining ivy, hung limp and motionless in the heat—in the hot, still, listening silence. Matt stared, listened and, after a few moments, called.

"Amelia," he called softly. He stopped to listen and then called again.

No answer. Of course there wouldn't be. After all, it wasn't as if she actually lived there in the cabin. He had to admit that the chances she would be there at any particular moment were pretty slim. Sitting down on a stone block that had once been a part of the church wall, he went over all the possibilities.

All the what-to-do-next possibilities. He could cross the ball field and risk his neck trying to get across the swamp. And then what? Go up and knock on the front door of the Palace and ask to see Amelia? As if!

Or he could just stay where he was, sitting there sweltering and sweating for an hour or two, just hoping that she might show up. Or . . .

It was then, while he was still sitting on the stone, that he happened to notice a glint of gold among the dead leaves that covered the floor of the path. Dropping to his knees, he brushed the leaves aside, and there it was—Amelia's locket on its gold chain. The locket on a broken golden chain, and right next to it—a small silver-colored key. A key to what? And then suddenly he knew.

Putting the locket and chain in his pocket, but holding the key in his hand, he hurried back to the side entrance. Inside the doorway he paused for only a moment and then, without letting himself stop to think, he went on along the interior wall and on through the sagging door of Old Tom's cabin.

Nothing had changed since he'd been there before. There were no changes in the rusted stove or in the rocking chair with its broken rocker, and the chewed-up bone was still lying right where, or very close to where, he himself had dropped it. And the trunk . . .

And then he was on his knees beside the old trunk. The dome-shaped lid encased in stamped metal was unchanged—and the shiny padlock still hung from the hasp. Telling himself it wouldn't fit, wouldn't be the right one, Matt reached out, tried the key—and the padlock fell open. The trunk was unlocked. Without his willing them to, in fact while he was trying to tell them not to, his hands reached out and raised the lid.

A kind of partition, a deep wooden tray, filled the top part of the trunk. A tray that was full of . . . hats? One on top of the other. Matt lifted them out one by one. Large floppy old-fashioned hats made of shiny materials, elaborately decorated with velvet ribbons and clusters of silky flowers. And each of them draped in clouds of heavy white veiling. Matt stared long and hard at the hats before he laid them aside and lifted out the wooden tray.

The bottom section of the trunk was much deeper and it was completely full of—dresses. Long dresses made of shiny silky materials, with cuffs and collars made of lace. Matt took two of the dresses out of the trunk, held them up one at a time, and looked them over carefully. A dress of filmy white material, and then a blue one, a pale misty blue. Staring at the blue dress, Matt remembered what Red Sinclair had said about the ghost his friend had seen, and the dress she'd been wearing. Pale blue, he'd said, and lacy. That was exactly what Mr. Sinclair had said. Matt was sure of it. He swallowed hard, almost a gulp, before he quickly folded the dresses, put them back in the trunk, put the hats back in the tray and placed it over the dresses. Then he closed the lid, fastened the padlock and slowly got to his feet.

Twenty-two

Twenty-two

What did it mean? What did a trunk full of old-fashioned hats and dresses mean? Maybe not much, except that it was exactly the kind of clothing the ghost of Rathburn Park had been described as wearing; and that he'd seen Amelia wear too. And then there was the fact that the key Amelia had carried on a chain around her neck opened the padlock on the trunk. And another thing to consider was what Brett Hardacre had said about there not being any kid named Amelia Rathburn who went to school in Timber City. And what Brett's grandmother, who ought to know, said about who lived, and who didn't live, in the Palace.

Matt found himself wondering if Amelia was just a kid who liked to pretend to be a ghost. Maybe even who only pretended to be a Rathburn. That could mean she didn't really live in the Palace, but there was the fact that she had taken Matt there, and obviously knew all about the old mansion and everything in it.

For a while, for quite a long time actually, Matt went on standing in the same spot in the middle of Old Tom's cabin. And then for another long spell, he sat in Old Tom's rocking chair, still thinking and wondering. He didn't remember actually sitting down, and he hadn't realized how long he'd been there, when he happened to glance at his watch. He jumped to his feet, whispering, "Wow, I got to get going."

A minute or two later he was hurriedly pushing his bike down the trail, while reminding himself to check to see if there was anyone close enough to notice, before he ducked out under the No Trespassing sign. Fortunately, nobody was anywhere near.

As a matter of fact, there was no one in sight at all. Even the two cars that had been on the far side of the parking lot were gone. Matt was swinging his leg up over the bicycle seat when he stopped in midswing, paralyzed with amazement.

Only a few yards away from where he was still standing on one leg, a small, cloud-colored dog trotted out of the forest and started across the parking lot. Trotted, and then stopped to look back, as if inviting Matt to follow him. Dropping his bike, stumbling over it and struggling to regain his balance, Matt ran after the dog. But although he ran his fastest, the dog was still several yards ahead of him when it disappeared among the trees at the other edge of the parking lot. Matt ran into the park, and stopped. No dog. No dog anywhere. He went on more slowly then, looking frantically from side to side as he went, looking everywhere.

He had passed the playground, and then several barbecue pits surrounded by tables, and there was still no dog. But this time he wasn't going to give up so easily. Hurrying on, he was almost to where a service road formed the boundary between the park and the open forest when he saw it. Saw not a small dog, but a large pickup truck.

Way down under the trees, a beat-up old pickup that had once been painted purple was parked on the shoulder of the road. Matt stopped and stared in a state of confused alarm that quickly turned into a scary premonition. A feeling that something awful was happening, or was about to. Trying to grin, he made an effort to shake it off.

What's wrong with you? he asked himself. It's just an old pickup. Might be anybody's. Except that it probably wasn't just anybody's, and who it really belonged to was almost certain to be a kid named Lance Layton.

Matt's next impulse was to run back to the parking lot, jump on his bike and get out of there as fast as he could, but something kept him nailed to the spot while questions started chasing each other through his mind. Questions, for instance, like what was Lance Layton's truck doing on a deserted service road on the Saturday afternoon when he was supposedly leaving to drive to the coast on the trip that Matt's brother had insisted he was going on, even though Mom and Dad said he couldn't? And then an even more urgent question, was Justin Hamilton in that truck, right then? At that very moment?

Without wanting to do it, in fact with one part of his mind definitely warning him not to, Matt started toward the truck. One more question did occur to him while he was on the way there. A question that went What do you think you're doing, Matt Hamilton? If Justin is there with Lance, what do you think you can do about it?

He certainly didn't have the answer to that one. Even after he got to the truck, and was standing there right beside it, the only answer he'd come up with was But he's my brother. Which under the circumstances didn't make a whole lot of sense.

The pickup was empty. No one was in the cab and except for a lot of junk, like bulgy garbage bags and oily car parts, the truck's bed was empty too. Matt was still staring over the tailgate when he began to hear voices. He couldn't see anyone at first because the chimney of a barbecue pit was blocking his view. But he recognized one of the voices. He ought to. It was his brother's. Matt's premonition had been right. Justin had come to the park in Lance Layton's truck.

All right, that wasn't so bad. Justin had gone out in Lance's truck, all right, but at least they hadn't started off to drive to the beach party. Matt was ready to hurry back to his bike when he realized the voices were getting louder. And suddenly there they were, coming around the barbecue pit and heading right for the truck—and for Matt.

There were three of them and one of them was Justin. One of the other guys was Lance Layton, and the third, the one Matt had never seen before, was a tall, broad-shouldered guy with tattooed arms and a partly shaved head. The tattooed guy was carrying what looked like a can of beer.

"Hey, Matt," Lance was shouting. "Hey, get away from that truck."

Matt backed away, calling, "That's all right. I'm going. I didn't touch anything."

Lance said something to the guy with the shaved head, who immediately threw down the beer can and started running. Even though Matt ran too he'd only managed a few steps when he was grabbed from behind, spun around and thrown to the ground. And then he was lying flat on his back on the road while the three of them stood over him. When he tried to sit up, the guy with the shaved head shoved him back down with his big black-booted foot. "So what's up, kid?" he said. "You spying on your big brother so you can rat and get everybody into a whole lot of trouble?"

Matt sat up again. He was saying, "No, I wasn't spying. I didn't even know—" when Lance stuck one of his feet out too and shoved Matt, kicked him actually, back down. And then Matt was lying there, trying to get his breath while the two big feet were pressing harder and harder on his chest.

But Justin was there too. Matt looked at his brother, stared at him, trying to ask him for help without putting it into words. But at first Justin's grin only seemed to say that he thought the whole thing was pretty funny. "So tell us, Hamster," Justin said, "how did you know where to find me? You been listening to my phone calls?"

"No. I didn't listen to your phone calls," Matt said, trying to keep his voice steady with no gurgling, tearful sounds. "I wasn't trying to find you either. I just happened to be following this dog and I just happened to notice the truck and—"

"Dog? What dog was that?" Justin's tone was sarcastic but at the same time he was pushing Lance out of the way and putting out his hand to pull Matt to his feet. But as soon as Matt was on his feet, the guy with the shaved head grabbed him away from Justin, spun him around and threw him down again, this time very hard.

Matt landed with a thud, whacking his head on the pavement so that there was a kind of explosion inside it, like fireworks on a dark night. And then for a moment nothing but darkness. But only for a moment and then he was coming back, beginning to be dimly aware of what had happened, and was still happening. Aware of the pain at the back of his head and—voices. Loud voices.

"Hey!" Justin was shouting. "Cut it out! Leave him alone. I can take care of him."

And then someone yelled, "Get your hands off me, Hamilton!" And there were other sounds, scuffling noises and thuds, and more thuds. And when Matt's eyes started working again, he saw his brother and the other guy fighting, throwing punches. Hard punches and kicks. The spinning darkness closed in again and when it lifted there was only his brother. Only Justin reaching down and pulling Matt to his feet and out of the way while the old purple pickup roared past them and down the road.

"You all right?" Justin asked.

"Yeah. I think so." Matt was still feeling a little woozy as he twisted his arm to look at his elbow, which was pretty raw, and then reached up to feel the back of his head. There was a lump and when he took his hand away there was blood on his fingers.

"Damn," Justin was muttering. "Goddamn goon." Matt knew that this time his brother wasn't swearing at him.

Twenty-three

Twenty-three

om was already home when Matt and Justin rode up the driveway on Matt's bicycle. Matt was on the seat hanging on to Justin, who had ridden all the way standing up. If Matt was supposed to be at home, grounded, which he actually was, Mom forgot to mention it when he walked into the kitchen with blood still smeared down his arm and all over the back of his shirt.

Grabbing him by his shoulders, she led him to a chair as if she thought he might be about to collapse. "What happened, darling?" she kept saying. "What on earth happened to you?"

But Matt only said, "Hey, I'm all right. It's not as bad as it looks. But you better turn me loose, Mom, or things are really going to get messy. I need to go to the bathroom, real bad."

It worked. Mom let him go, which left it up to Justin to fill in the details before Matt came back from the bathroom. Came back after a quick detour to his room, where he hid Amelia's locket and key at the back of his underwear drawer. He didn't hear Justin's explanation, but when he got back to the kitchen Mom was on the phone to Mrs. Nelson, who lived next door and who happened to be a registered nurse.

Dad got home just as Mrs. Nelson was arriving and for a while a lot of people were talking at once and looking at the back of Matt's head. And then the nurse was telling Mom and Dad a lot of stuff about what Matt should and shouldn't do for the next few hours, like not going to sleep and being sure to say so if he started feeling dizzy. Everybody kept asking him how he felt, but no one asked him how it had happened, which was a good thing because he wouldn't have known what to say. At least he wouldn't have until he heard Mom explaining that Matt had taken a bad fall on his bike and Justin had rescued him and brought him home.

Justin got a lot of attention that night at the dinner table. Good attention. Like he was some kind of hero. Of course Matt got some attention too, but who wouldn't if they were wrapped up in more bandages than an Egyptian mummy, not to mention the limp that he'd thrown in as an added special effect? But the attention Matt got was more like he was some kind of world-class victim who was lucky to be alive, and especially lucky to have a lifesaving big brother to come to his rescue. Matt didn't mention Lance Layton and his pickup and neither did anyone else. In fact the whole "What Exactly Happened to the Hamster" mystery story didn't get nearly as much attention as Matt had been afraid it might.

The other reason that Matt's so-called accident didn't get as much attention as he might have expected was that Courtney kept changing the subject to the results of her latest allergy test and what they meant, which was that she wasn't nearly as allergic as she used to be.

"Isn't that frustrating?" Courtney said to Dad and anyone else she could get to listen. "I probably outgrew a lot of my allergies years ago and that doctor in Six Palms just didn't bother to retest me. And, Dad—listen, Dad. Dr. Rogers said I'm not allergic to dogs anymore, and, Dad . . . Listen, Dad, and Mom, too. I'm not. I know I'm not."

And when Mom started saying they shouldn't rush it and maybe they ought to wait to be sure, Courtney interrupted her.

"But I am sure," Courtney said. "I did my own test this afternoon. I spent the whole afternoon playing with Brittany's Taffy and her new puppies and look at me." Courtney breathed deeply. "See, no wheezing. No coughing."

The next topic of conversation was, of course, whether Courtney could have one of Taffy's puppies, a topic that the whole family got into and finally put to a kind of vote. A vote that wound up with a split decision. Three *yesses*, a *no*, and a *not now but maybe later*. You might think that, in a democracy, that would mean the *yesses* won, but not in a Hamilton-type democracy in which some votes counted more than others. After it became apparent that the *no* votes had won, Courtney started crying and left the table.

Later when Matt was waiting in the hall for Courtney to come out of the bathroom, Justin went past and said, "Hey, Hamster. Thanks a lot."

"Me? Thank me?" Matt made it into a question. "For . . . ?"

Justin grinned. "For keeping your mouth shut."

"Oh, that," Matt said. "I thought you meant for letting you save my life."

"Oh, that." Justin's grin was pretty uncomplicated for once. "Anytime, kid."

Matt spent a pretty lousy night, what with having a real doozy of a headache and having to be awakened several times by his mom and dad to be sure he was just asleep and not in some kind of coma. He was still in bed the next morning and not in a very good mood when Justin barged into the room.

Just one loud thud and Justin came on in, the way he always did. But he didn't look the way he always did. There was something about the way Justin looked that made Matt forget all about his bad mood and sit straight up in bed. "What is it? What's the matter?"

For a long moment Justin just stared at him, and then he turned away toward the window, shaking his head and making strange meaningless gestures with both hands.

"Justin, tell me." Matt jumped out of bed and hurried across the room. "What's the matter?"

Justin shook his head hard and went on shaking it for a long time before he started to talk. "They're in the hospital, both of them. Dead maybe, the paper didn't say exactly."

"Dead? Wh-who? Who's dead?" Matt stammered.

"Lance. And Rocky. They went off a cliff. Last night on their way to the party."

"Off—off a cliff?" Matt's voice wavered and then almost disappeared. "How . . . ? Who . . . ?"

Justin collapsed on the window seat and Matt did too. For a long time neither of them said anything. Leaning forward with his elbows on his knees and his chin in his hands, Justin stared at the floor, and Matt stared at Justin. It wasn't until a kind of eternity had passed that Matt asked, "How did it happen? Did anybody see it happen?"

Justin shook his head. "Nobody knows. They're still unconscious." Shaking his head again, he said, "Lance is a good driver. It must have been the beer."

"The beer?"

"Yeah. That's what they . . ." He paused, blinked and swallowed hard before he went on. "That's what *we* were doing at the park. Rocky showed up with three six-packs, and Lance didn't want to take the stuff to the coast in the truck because the cops know him and they're always stopping him, and if they found the beer cans . . ." Justin shrugged. "So he decided we'd stop off at the park and—get rid of it before we left."

"Get rid of the beer?" Matt said. "Oh yeah, I get it. Get rid of it—that way."

Then came another long spell of silence before Justin got up slowly and went to the door. He turned then and looked back at Matt. He was trying to do his cool one-sided grin, only both sides of his mouth looked kind of sick.

"Thanks again, Hamster," he said. "Thanks for saving my life."

"Anytime, kid," Matt said.

Twenty-four
Twenty-four

The next few days were kind of up and down. Some good moments and some others that were pretty awful. Like Sunday, for instance.

On Sunday the whole family was talking about the accident, or in the case of Matt and Justin, mostly listening while other people talked about it. Both Mom and Dad had a lot to say to Justin on the subject, some of it where Matt could hear the conversation and some of it where he couldn't. But the part he did hear made Matt feel really bad for Justin.

What Mom actually was saying to Justin was a lot of stuff about how sorry she was about what had happened to his friends, but how glad she and Dad were that Justin had had the good sense to change his mind about going with them that night. Matt was watching his brother's face while Mom was talking and he could tell how miserable Justin was feeling. Mom must have seen it too, but she must have thought it was just because he was worried about Lance.

Sometime during the morning Mom called the Laytons

to say how sorry they all were about what had happened, and how Lance and his friend were in their thoughts and prayers. And then during lunch she told everybody what Mrs. Layton had told her.

The news was that Lance was improving but that Rocky was still in a coma, and the doctors were afraid he might be paralyzed. Both of the boys had been tested for alcohol consumption, Mrs. Layton said. The results hadn't been established yet, but she was worried about it because Lance was the one who had been driving.

When Mom told about the alcohol tests, Justin looked at Matt and went on looking. But what Matt saw in his brother's face wasn't a threat, or even a signal that he was asking Matt to go on keeping his mouth shut. The only thing Justin's eyes seemed to be saying was how sick he was feeling, and a minute later he left the table without finishing his lunch. By the next day the news from the hospital was that Lance and Rocky were doing a little better, but that Lance was in serious trouble with the police because of the results of the alcohol tests.

The other thing Matt kept thinking about during the next few days was Amelia, wondering where she was and if he was ever going to see her again. And what would happen when he did? It didn't really make a whole lot of difference where she was at the moment, however, because he knew without asking that he wouldn't be allowed anywhere near his bicycle until . . . Well, until he got rid of the bandages, at least. It was too bad, though.

Too bad because . . . Well, because he had a whole lot of questions he needed to ask her, and things to tell her about. One thing he really needed to tell her was what had happened that Saturday afternoon, because there was an important part of it that he couldn't discuss with anyone else. And that was the part about Rover. No one else would believe for a minute that, if it hadn't been for Rover, Matt wouldn't have stopped to look around and notice the pickup way down there on the service road. And if he hadn't, Justin probably would have been in the truck when it went over the cliff.

It was only a few days later that in spite of the powerful *No* votes, Courtney came home with a puppy. Matt didn't know how she managed it, except he was pretty sure the tears had something to do with it. Anybody who could cry that hard and look that good while she was doing it could get around a whole lot of negative votes.

Anyway, Matt was sitting on the front steps when Courtney and the puppy arrived, and it was a pretty exciting moment. Courtney was—well, you can imagine what a person would be feeling like who had spent her whole childhood grieving because she couldn't have a dog, and then suddenly could—and did. The grinning Greek mask didn't even touch it.

The puppy, whom Courtney had named Dusty, was a few weeks old and he looked like no particular brand of dog that Matt knew about. His mother, Taffy, looked a little like some kind of spaniel, but the word was that Dusty's father had been more of a terrier, and the result was something that looked like a small, lively haystack. Obviously a mutt, but a mutt with a pedigreed personality according to Courtney, and Matt agreed she was right about that.

Matt and Courtney went on sitting on the front steps

while the puppy played on the lawn, chasing a tennis ball and running in circles and falling over his own big feet.

"And he has another special kind of pedigree," Courtney told Matt. "A Timber City pedigree." And when Matt asked what that was, she went on, "Well, according to Brittany's mom, Taffy's ancestors have lived in Timber City for a whole lot of generations. Like maybe ten or twelve. I mean just about every family who has lived here for a long time has owned one of Taffy's ancestors. And even though they're no special breed anymore, they're all especially brilliant."

It was just about then that the puppy started running in circles, chasing his tail. He went on chasing it until he ran headfirst into the gatepost and fell over. When he sat back up, he was looking kind of cockeyed and woozy.

"Yeah," Matt said, grinning. "Real brilliant, all right."

Matt and Courtney sat on the front steps watching the puppy for a long time that day. Every few minutes he would run back where they were sitting, and now and then Courtney would pick him up and hold him on her lap. Matt played with Dusty too, but Courtney asked Matt not to pick him up, at least not for a few days, because he was her dog and she wanted him to imprint on her.

"Brittany's mother knows a lot about raising dogs," Courtney told Matt, "and she says that when a puppy is first adopted, it needs to pick out one person to imprint on. And he *is* my puppy."

Matt got the picture. But even if Dusty wasn't actually his, it was still pretty cool having a dog in the immediate family after so many years without one.

As the days passed some things seemed to be changing for the better, at least for some people. Justin started playing baseball with the Timber City Tigers and he got to be a pitcher right away, just like back in Six Palms. Around home he'd started talking more too. Especially to Matt. He talked to Matt about baseball almost every day, like about his great new split-fingered pitch, and a couple of times he even talked about the book on Daniel Boone that Matt was reading.

And Courtney had a lot of new stuff to do too, like playing with Dusty, and going swimming and partying with people Brittany had introduced her to.

But for Matt himself nothing had changed all that much. There were still some sleepless nights and some lonely days, which he tended to spend staring into space while he thought about Rathburn Park and who and what he might, or might not, see the next time he was allowed to go there.

But finally, on a foggy Tuesday morning in late August, Matt's last bandage came off and he got permission to ride his bicycle to the park again.

The weather had definitely changed. Halfway down the drive Matt stopped and went back for a jacket and it wasn't until then that he remembered the key and locket. As he fished them out from under his socks and boxer shorts he told himself that if he couldn't find Amelia he might at least be able to find a way to leave them where she would be sure to find them.

The fog became deeper and damper as Matt pedaled toward the park. Along the road, houses and barns and trees that had always been in plain view were now no more than vague shadows, and here and there ghostly white wisps drifted across dips in the road. Inside the park the change was even more noticeable. Swirling clouds hung low over the deserted parking lot, and all around it the treetops seemed to rise out of a foggy ocean. On the narrow path that led to the ruined church, a heavy mist almost like rain dripped on Matt's head and trickled down the back of his neck.

Just as he'd been warning himself to expect, no one answered when he called from the side entrance of the church. Called Amelia, and then Rover, and then Amelia again. No answer. So what next? On the one hand, he would be breaking his promise again if he went in, but on the other, he had a pretty good excuse this time. Two excuses, actually. The first one concerned finding a good place to leave the locket, and the second one could be about needing to get in out of the rain. Rehearsing how he could explain very quickly if Amelia happened to show up, he slithered in along the wall, pulled open the door and once again stepped into Old Tom's cabin.

This time there was a change, an important one, and Matt noticed it the moment the door closed behind him. The trunk was unlocked. The lid was closed, the latch was down, but there was no padlock. The moment he saw it, even before he crossed the room and squatted down in front of the trunk, he knew the difference was an important one. Important, and somehow threatening. Wishing he didn't have to, but knowing he did, he reached out and raised the lid.

The trunk was empty. No hats or dresses. Nothing except a tiny wisp of a peacock feather that had once been attached to a fancy old hat. Picking up the wisp of feather, Matt knelt there staring at it for only a minute before he knew what he was going to do next. Knew, not *why* exactly, but only *what*. He was going to go to the Rathburn Palace to look for Amelia. *Why* he was going to do it was a question he'd have to find an answer to later.

Slamming the door of the cabin behind him, he almost stumbled into the booby trap pit as he hurried around the wall. Then he ran in an uncomfortable crouch through the drizzly tunnel path, and continued to run, at top speed now, across the parking lot and the ballpark. He didn't slow down until he reached the edge of the swamp.

Twenty-five
Twenty-five

The swamp. As he stood on the slimy bank looking out at the murky water, its scattered reedy islands barely visible in the thick fog, Matt tried to remember not Frankie and his awful fate, but Amelia's assurance that it was easy if you just remembered to keep moving. Then he was moving, jumping from one squashy clump of reeds to the next, and on again, without pausing even for a second. And very soon he was clambering up the other bank and stopping for only a moment of self-congratulation before making his way to the gate that led onto the Palace grounds.

Still feeling unusually confident because of his easy triumph over the swamp, he was halfway through the overgrown garden before he stopped to look up. Up to the clutter of fancy towers and balconies, and then down to where, not far away now, a broad stairway led up to the wide veranda and the Palace's grand double-doored entryway.

What did he think he was doing? Was he really planning to march right up and ring the doorbell? And then what? When someone came to the door, would he ask to see a girl named Amelia—a girl who, according to Mrs. Hardacre, didn't exist? Or if she did exist, maybe not in the way most ordinary people did.

Turning back, Matt scooted into the underbrush, squatted down and began to give the matter some serious thought. It didn't take long to decide that the grand front entrance would not be a possibility. Instead—what? A few minutes later he was making his way around the house to where a broken basement window could be easily opened if you had been shown, and remembered, how to do it.

Matt did remember how, but it wasn't a very easy thing to do with no one to hold the window open as he scooted through. It was with a scraped knee and a slightly banged head and elbow that he finally made his way down to the basement floor—and complete darkness.

He'd forgotten about that. Forgotten the darkness—but fortunately . . . Fishing in his pocket, he brought out a key chain that held his house key, a small screwdriver *and* a tiny flashlight—the kind that is supposed to give you just enough light to find a keyhole on a dark night. But not really enough, he soon discovered, to light your way through a maze of underground storage rooms. Bumbling along, bumping into chests, boxes and barrels, Matt tried not to recall the nightmare he'd had about being in the Palace basement and stumbling over the bodies of dead and almost dead animals.

He made his way through several rooms that he vaguely remembered. The one that smelled of aging wine, and the ones where large pieces of furniture sat around covered by ghostly white sheets. He had just passed what looked to be a large sheet-draped armoire when, with no warning at all, rough clawlike fingers reached out from nowhere and grabbed him by the shoulders.

"Let me go. Let me go," Matt gasped. Shocked and terror-stricken, he ducked and squirmed, trying to pull away. But the big hands were strong and very firm.

"No chance, kid," a deep, rumbling voice said. "You're coming with me." And then, with one big hand still on Matt's shoulder and the other twisting his left arm up behind his back, Matt was being pushed up some stairs, through a door and out into a hall. Into the immense grand hallway with its gilded pillars, stained-glass windows and gold-framed mirrors.

It wasn't until then that Matt saw the large, shaggy-haired man who had captured him. Saw him not face to face, but in several mirrors as they made their way down the hall and then up another wide flight of stairs.

Matt tried once or twice to plead his case, saying things like, "Hey, mister. Please let me go. I'm not a robber or anything. I was just . . ."

"Yeah? Just what?"

"Just trying to talk to Amelia. Please, just ask her. Ask Amelia. She'll tell you who I am."

There was no answer except for a snorting laugh. "That's a good one. Well, that's what we're going to do, kid. That's exactly where we're going." And then the shaggy old man was knocking on a door. A sharp-faced woman in a white uniform opened it and Matt was pushed forward into a room.

The large room was dimly lit and smelled of antiseptics and stale perfume. There was a bed at one end of the room, and at the other the sharp-faced woman who had opened the door had moved back to stand next to a wheelchair. And in the chair a thin old woman dressed in shiny black was frowning sternly in Matt's direction. The woman's face was deeply wrinkled, but her small dark eyes were bright and quick. Her frown deepened as she said, "Well, well, Ernie. What have we here?"

"A boy, ma'am," the big old man said. "Found him creeping around in the basement. Said he wanted to talk to . . ." He paused and chuckled. "To talk to Amelia."

"Did you indeed? In our basement?" She turned to Matt. "You have some explaining to do, young man," she said. "You might begin by telling us why you wanted to talk to me."

For a moment all Matt could do was shake his head. "No. No, ma'am. Not you. I wanted to talk to . . ." He held out his hand to indicate someone about his height. "To the girl who lives here."

"The girl? What girl would that be?" And then suddenly, "Ah yes, I think I understand." She turned toward the woman in the white uniform. "Freda," she said, "do you know anything about this? Could this concern your Dolly?"

The woman named Freda shook her head. "I don't think so, ma'am. Don't see how it could. But . . ." Her eyes narrowed and so did her thin lips. "But we'll soon find out." She turned away, hurried across the room and out the door, and a moment later Matt heard a voice that sounded vaguely familiar. A harsh, angry voice calling, "Dolly. Dolly. Dolly."

They waited, with the big man still gripping Matt's

shoulders and the woman in the wheelchair still looking at him curiously. Now and then she asked questions like "What is your name, boy?"

"Matt, ma'am." No point in lying now. They could easily find out who he was. "Matthew Hamilton."

"And where is your home, Matthew?"

"In Timber City, ma'am. On Rathburn Avenue."

"And tell me how you managed to get into my basement."

That was harder. He didn't want to blame it on . . . to say who it was who had shown him how to get in through the broken window. He was still stammering, trying to find something to say that would be believable, when suddenly the door to the hall flew open with a bang and two people burst into the room. The bigger one was the woman in the white uniform and the other was—Amelia. The wild-eyed girl who called herself Amelia was struggling to pull free from the woman's grasp.

The same Amelia for sure and certain, even though she looked different and somehow smaller in jeans and a T-shirt, and in the midst of a fierce struggle with a large, determined-looking woman.

"Let go of me, Grandma," Amelia was saying. "I didn't do anything. Why do I have to—" It wasn't until then that she looked up and saw Matt and for a second seemed to freeze. To freeze, to stare at Matt as if in horror and then to go limp. A moment later she was lying on the floor in a silent, motionless heap while the woman in the white uniform and the shaggy-haired man bent over her. The other woman, the one in the wheelchair, was also moving her chair toward them, looking startled and concerned.

Suddenly left to his own devices, Matt moved closer, watching the woman in white roll Amelia onto her back, feel her pulse and pat her cheeks. He was worried too, at least at first, but before long he began to suspect something. To suspect that maybe Amelia wasn't as unconscious as she looked. He didn't know why, at least not exactly, except that he had reason to know that where Amelia was concerned, things usually weren't what they seemed.

"Smelling salts," the woman in the chair was calling. "Get my smelling salts, Freda."

It was then, while the woman in white was jumping to her feet and rushing out of the room, and the man was adjusting the other Amelia's wheelchair, that Matt moved closer and whispered, "Amelia. Hey, Amelia. It's me."

And Amelia whispered back. Opening one eye, she barely mouthed, "Get out of here. Run!" And Matt did.

Easing toward the door, he tiptoed out, down the stairs, down the long hallway and another grander flight of stairs to some huge double doors. He managed to pull one of them open, shot out across the veranda and on down to the ground. He stopped then just long enough to glance back over his shoulder, to listen for sounds of pursuit. Nothing. He went on running.

Twenty-six
Twenty-six

With the Palace behind him, and soon afterward the swamp as well, Matt's pace finally slowed. As he went on, walking slowly, it was only his mind that was racing, worrying, puzzling and questioning. And beginning to come up with some possible answers.

As he walked across the ball field he concentrated on asking himself who Amelia, or whoever, really was. By the time he'd reached the parking lot he had decided that she was not Amelia at all, probably not even a Rathburn. She was probably the granddaughter of the nurse woman called Freda. And her name was . . . It didn't seem possible that her name was actually Dolly.

The fog had lifted somewhat and as he passed the beginning of the path that led to the graveyard Matt suddenly stopped to stare. To stare down the path and then, without knowing why, to turn down it. A few minutes later he was kneeling in the grass beside Old Tom's grave—and the other grave that was probably Rover's.

Pushing the weeds and ivy away from Rover's tombstone, he began to whisper. "So that's it, Rover," he said.

"So she's just a liar. A girl who likes to pretend she's some-body more important than she really is." He shrugged angrily. "Well, she sure fooled me."

He was still feeling angry, at the would-be Amelia, and at himself, too, for having been fooled for so long, when he suddenly jumped to his feet and whirled around to face the path. He'd heard something—the sound of running feet. The sound quickly grew louder and Matt was still frozen with surprise and fright when Amelia burst into view. Amelia—or whoever. Sliding to a stop, she stared at him, and then slowly turned in a circle like she was looking for something or someone else.

"So," Matt finally managed to say. "Are you all right? Did you faint, or what?"

She shrugged. "Nothing happened to me. I was just pretending. I'm good at pretending." She grinned. "It worked, didn't it? They thought I was . . ." She shrugged again and went on, "I don't know what they thought, but right after you escaped I did too. I just jumped up and ran. And as soon as I got outside I started looking for you, but you'd already gone." She stopped and once again turned in a circle.

Matt was feeling angry again. "So," he said. "So you're not Amelia after all. Okay. What should I call you?"

She turned toward him angrily and then shrugged, curling her lower lip. "Right," she said. "My real name is Dolly Davis. And sometimes I live with my grandmother, who is Freda Davis, R.N. As in Registered Nurse." She shook her head. "Can you believe it? Do I look like a Dolly to you?"

Matt found it hard to keep from grinning. "Well, no, you don't, actually," he said. "So what should I call you?"

"I don't care." Clenching a fist, she shook it threateningly. "But it better not be Dolly."

"Okay. Okay." He was grinning now. "I guess I'll just go on calling you Amelia. Okay? At least when no one else is around."

She stared at him with narrowed eyes for a moment before she unclenched her fist and nodded thoughtfully. "Yeah, you can do that. That's okay."

"But how about when school starts? What will I call you at school?"

Amelia laughed. "Well, don't worry about that. I don't go to school in Timber City. I never have. I go to school in Seattle."

"In Seattle. How can you live here and go to school in Seattle?"

She shrugged. "It's easy. I only live here in the summer. See, my mother works for a ship company and most of the year she works in Seattle. And we live right downtown in an apartment building. But in the summer she works on ships that go back and forth to Alaska and I can't go with her. So I get sent here for three months to stay with my grandmother. I do it every year. This was my fourth summer in the Palace."

"Wow!" Matt said. "Lucky you." Turning to look toward the Palace, he narrowed his eyes, picturing what it would be like to actually live in a huge, old, historic place like—

"Yeah, sure." Amelia broke into his daydream. "But it would be more fun if the rest of them weren't such a bunch of grouches. And if they, if any of them, liked having me around." Suddenly her voice was shaky and her eyes blinked rapidly.

Not knowing what else to say, Matt could only think to ask, "The rest of them? At the Palace, you mean?"

She swallowed hard and then shrugged. "Yeah, my granny and old Miss Rathburn and Ernie and Irma."

"Irma?"

"She's the cook. Ernie's her husband. None of them like having me around." She laughed in a sarcastic way. "Oh well, I'm used to it. My mom feels the same way. She likes getting rid of me every summer. She liked me when I was her cute little Dolly, but now . . ." She stopped and turned her face away.

Matt was thinking that he understood. He knew what it was like to feel kind of in everybody's way. Suddenly he thought of something that might help take her mind off her problems.

"Hey." He dug into his jacket pocket and held out the locket and key on the golden chain. "Look what I found. It's yours, isn't it?"

For a long moment she stared at what Matt was holding before she slowly reached out and took it. And then for another long moment she stared at what was in her hand—before she sank down into a crouching position. With her head bent low, she began to cry. Real heartbroken, shuddering, gasping sobs. And standing over her, Matt wondered what he had done—and what he could do now.

"Hey," he said finally. "Don't do that. I just thought you'd like to have it back. I found it on the path."

The crying went on for a while and then gradually began to lessen. At last Amelia raised her teary face, stared at Matt and asked, "The key? Do you know what the key is for?"

Reluctantly, Matt nodded.

"And what was in it? You know what I keep in the trunk?"

Matt nodded again. "Well, yeah. I guess I do."

She cried again, even harder.

"Look," Matt said. "It's all right. I won't tell anybody."

The sobs grew softer and finally she lifted her head and sighed deeply. "It doesn't matter. Even if you don't tell, it's all over. I won't be able to do it again. Not with somebody knowing. Even if it's only—" Her smile was still painful, but a little bit teasing, too. "If it's only you."

"Do what again? You won't be able to do what?"

Her sigh was sad and resigned. "Be Amelia. It won't work now that someone knows. It's all over."

"Why won't it work?" Matt said. "Tell me about it. About being Amelia."

She shook her head.

Matt took a deep breath. "It won't matter that I know. Look. I'll tell you about . . ." He grinned. "About being Robin Hood. And Alexander the Great. And Napoleon." He shoved his hand under one side of his jacket and put on a stern, dignified expression. "I've done it all my life. And sometimes I dress up too. I used to have a great Napoleon outfit until my brother used it for grease rags."

She giggled weakly, shook her head, nodded, sighed and began to talk. "See, there's this beautiful painting of one of the Amelias in the library. The one who died in 1877. And then, in the attic, I found out all about her. She died when she was only sixteen and her parents put all her stuff away in the attic. All her clothing and her diaries and like that. And I started reading the diaries and then . . ."

She paused, sighed and went on. "And then I started being Amelia. Every summer I take some of her clothing to Old Tom's cabin and I go there to put it on. And then I'm Amelia most of the summer."

Matt nodded, grinning. "You're Amelia—and you must be the ghost of Rathburn Park, too. Did you know that ghost stories have been going around about the park and the graveyard? Like maybe people saw you and thought you were a ghost?"

Amelia looked sneakily pleased. "Yeah. I thought so. I mean there were a couple of times when I had to run to get away. Once they probably would have caught me, but I ran across the swamp and got away. And there was one time when some little boys were trying to steal a tombstone and I scared them half to death."

Matt laughed and after a moment Amelia did too. But then he remembered something. "Hey," he said, "I stopped at the cabin today . . ." He grinned guiltily. "And I went in." He paused, watching her warily. "You know, just to find a place to leave the locket, and the trunk was . . ."

She nodded. "Yeah, it was empty."

"But how did you do it? Without the key?"

"There's another key," she said.

"Oh sure," Matt said. "But why? Why did you take everything out?"

"Because I'm leaving," she said. "My mother is coming for me tomorrow. I'm going back to Seattle."

Matt stared at her, feeling . . . Well, not feeling good. Stared and went on staring. "What?" she said finally. "What's the matter?"

"I don't know. I just wish . . . I wish you weren't going."

After a while she nodded and said, "Yeah. I wish it too." She nodded again. "We could write to each other. I know your address. I looked it up. And next summer I'll be back."

"Sure," Matt said. "Next summer you can be Amelia again and . . ."

She giggled. "And you can be Robin Hood." Her giggle turned into a sigh. "I have to go now." She was halfway down the path when she stopped and turned back.

"What is it?" Matt asked. "What are you looking for?"

Amelia's eyes narrowed for a second and then opened extra wide. "For Rover. Didn't you see him? Just before I got here?"

Matt shook his head.

"Well, he came in here," she said. "How do you think I found you?" She turned and then started running and Matt didn't try to follow.

Twenty-seven

Twenty-seven

Matt didn't really believe that Amelia had seen Rover that day in the park. He did look around some—in the park and on his way home, too, but the only dog he saw was an unfriendly German shepherd.

During the next week, the last one before school started, he thought about Rover a lot, and he even managed two short trips to the park and to Old Tom's cabin. But he didn't see, or hear, anything the least bit extraordinary. The trunk was still empty and the dog bone was still in the same spot under the cot.

Then on Sunday evening after he'd gone to bed he was sure he heard a dog barking, a deep distant sound that definitely wasn't Dusty. He jumped up and ran to the window but nothing was moving on the lawn or at the edge of the forest. After a while a flock of geese flew over and there were some honking sounds that might have been what he'd heard—but maybe not.

But once school started there was so much other stuff

to think about. The kid named Brett was in two of Matt's classes and he was still friendly, and some of the teachers were pretty okay. Like for instance a gym teacher who didn't let kids choose up teams and embarrass the ones who were natural-born klutzes by not choosing them till last.

At home Courtney was in one of the longest-lasting good moods Matt could remember. She liked being in high school and every day after school she was busy taking care of Dusty, when she wasn't going places with people Brittany had introduced her to. Particularly with Brittany's cousin, Brad, who was fifteen and, according to Courtney, *big-time gorgeous*. And as for Justin, he was still being more like the big brother he used to be before he got to be such a hotshot teenager. Mom and Dad were as busy as usual. Matt was feeling okay. Nothing special, but okay.

September was almost over when Matt checked the mail and found a letter from Seattle addressed to Matt Hamilton. The name in the return address corner was a big scribbled capital letter that could have been almost anything but certainly looked more like an *A* than a *D*. Just the *A*, or perhaps *D* and then the last name—*Davis*. He stuck the envelope inside his shirt and went to his room.

Sure enough, the letter was from Amelia and she said she was in Seattle but that she was definitely going to be back at the Palace for a short visit at Christmas and, of course, all next summer.

"So I'll see you then," she wrote, "and we can both look

out for Rover. I have a feeling we're going to see a lot of him."

Matt was still lying on his bed a little later, not writing yet but thinking about what he would say in his letter to Amelia. It was still in the planning stage when there was a knock on his door and Courtney came in. She was wearing a sharp-looking new outfit and a lot more makeup than usual, and she was carrying Dusty under one arm and his dog bed under the other.

"Look," she said, "I was wondering if you'd baby-sit my poor doggy for a while tonight." She dropped the dog bed in the corner of the room and put Dusty in it.

Matt sat up and looked at the about-to-be-deserted puppy. Dusty wasn't looking very happy. His ears were droopy and he seemed to be shivering.

"Is something wrong with him?" Matt asked.

"I don't think so," Courtney said. She squatted down in front of the dog bed for a minute and then stood up and looked at Matt. "He's all right. It's just that I've been gone quite a bit lately and . . ."

"Yeah, that's for sure," Matt said. "Enter Big-Time-Gorgeous Brad—exit puppy."

Courtney sighed. "You sound just like Mom." Then she blew a kiss and went out the door.

Matt went on lying on his bed with his chin on his hands, looking at Dusty. And the little dog went on shivering and looking sad.

"Too bad," Matt told the puppy. "Too bad you didn't come along a little sooner. Like pre-Brad."

He grinned but the puppy didn't grin back. After a

while Matt sat up and patted the bed beside where he was sitting. "All right, Dusty," he said. "Come on up here."

The dog stayed where he was. "Dusty," Matt called. "Come on, Dusty." Nothing happened.

"Wow," Matt said, "stay there then." Going to his desk, he got a pen and a notebook and switched off the overhead light. Then he got back on the bed, turned on his reading lamp, and started to answer Amelia's letter. But after *Dear Amelia* he couldn't decide what to say next. He hadn't gotten any farther when the puppy started to whine.

Matt looked up, and then looked again. The little dog was sitting up now and in the dimmer light his fur looked different, softer and cloudy gray.

Matt stared for a moment before he whispered, "Rover? Hey, Rover."

The puppy sat up, cocking his head and lolling his tongue. He looked, Matt thought, like someone who'd just told a joke or played a trick on somebody. Then he trotted across the room, jumped up on the bed, turned around several times and settled down with his chin on Matt's ankle. Matt grinned at him and he grinned back.

"So," Matt said, "what are you telling me? That you're some kind of Rover clone or relative? Or maybe that some people are sure to get a Rover when they really need one? Maybe that's it, or else . . ." He shrugged. "Or else the whole thing is just my crazy imagination again. Which is it?"

Rover wagged his tail, but he wasn't talking. Matt picked up his pen. "Wait till I tell Amelia," he said. "Till I tell her she was right. We're going to be seeing a lot of Rover next summer."

ZILPHA KEATLEY SNYDER has written many popular and award-winning books for young readers, including *The Egypt Game, The Headless Cupid* and *The Witches of Worm,* all Newbery Honor Books and ALA Notable Books. Her most recent novels are *Spyhole Secrets* and two novels about Gib Whittaker, *Gib Rides Home* and *Gib and the Gray Ghost,* which were inspired by stories her father told her about his childhood in a Nebraska orphanage.

Zilpha Keatley Snyder lives in Marin County, California.